WEDDING GHOST

Haunted Everly After

BOOK SIX

REGINA WELLING
ERIN LYNN

Wedding Ghost

ISBN- 978-1-953044-32-7

Cover design by: L. Vryhof

Interior design by: L. Vryhof

http://reginawelling.com

http://erinlynnwrites.com

First Edition

Printed in the U.S.A.

Table of Contents

Chapter One

"Calm down. I think you're ready." The old wooden chair behind Patrea's desk creaked as she leaned back. Hearing the sound, her eyes narrowed for a moment before she pulled her attention back to me.

"But what if," I began.

"You're ready."

"They might," I began again.

"You're ready." The chair creaked again as she leaned forward and pinned me with a look. "You're ready for whatever they throw at you."

With just under a week to go until the trial, I still couldn't figure out why the prosecuting attorney thought it was a good idea for me to testify against my ex-husband. Not because I had any intention of protecting him, but because I didn't know anything useful to the case. After my divorce, it became painfully clear that my position as Director of Development within his family's charitable foundation had sounded far more important than the position actually was.

"You say that, but then you tell me Paul's attorney plans to shred me on the stand." Was I worried? Far less than I probably should have been. "I don't even care as long as this is the end of my dealings with the Hastings family. This is the end, right?"

Sighing because I'd asked the same question more than once, Patrea nodded.

"Honestly, Ev, this whole trial is a farce. If Paul gets more than a slap on the wrist, I'll be shocked. Not with Reva as a handy scapegoat. His attorney will play him off as her unwitting dupe. Colin Peterson specializes in turning his guilty clients into victims, and there are plenty of witnesses to what Reva did to Paul. Peterson won't have any trouble making it stick."

"Then why do they need me at all?" It wasn't the first time I'd asked that, either.

She sighed and deadpanned, "Thurston made good on all the donation money Paul and Reva stole. Rumor is he even matched the funds out of his own pocket, so all the charities received double. That appeased the donors, and they've all decided to let bygones be bygones." It wasn't the first time she'd given me the same answer. "But the DA is grasping at straws."

"And I'm a straw. "

Early on in the judicial process, it looked like the DA's office would drop the charges against Paul. Instead, they'd tacked on a few more. Peterson managed to get the conspiracy to commit murder, attempted murder, and accessory to murder charges thrown out.

Call me small-minded and petty if you must. I won't argue the point. I'd have a hard time pulling that off because I still smile a little when I picture Paul naked and chained to a hotel-room bed by the guttersnipe tramp he'd dumped me for. I can't help myself. It's an excellent mental image.

This was after he and Reva tried to set me up to take the fall for embezzling funds and set the FBI on me. It was also after she showed up at my house and tried to murder me, so you can see why I might be a little bitter. I thought they both deserved to spend some time behind bars, but that didn't mean I had any concrete proof to offer the court.

The prosecuting attorney didn't seem to care about that particular detail.

"But you're ready," Patrea repeated. "All you have to do is tell the truth. Now, put it out of your head until Wednesday. And tell me what you think of these paint colors."

She gestured toward a wall featuring several splotches of gray in an attempt to change the subject, a feat easier said than done given how the trial date was something of a moving target. It had been moved up six months and then pushed forward by a week twice already. I just wanted the ordeal over with, but I dragged my attention back to the present and assessed the swaths of color.

"I'm leaning toward that one. It's called Shadow Gray." Patrea pointed to her choice. "It has a slightly warmer tone than the Cloud Gray." She gestured to another. "This one is even warmer, but there's a pink undertone I'm not sure about."

She'd just ordered me to tell the truth, so I did. "They all look exactly the same to me," I said.

"You're no help to me at all. They're clearly not the same." Just to be certain, Patrea snatched a set of reading glasses from the corner of her desk, shoved them on, and stuck her face close to the wall. I failed to hold back a grin as I watched her head swivel back and forth between the three splashes of color. "Shadow has more blue in it."

I'd have to take her word on it.

"Which one will go best with that mahogany partners desk in my back room? The one you've been drooling over ever since I showed you Catherine's stash." The former owner of my house liked to collect things. Lots and lots of things.

"No."

"What do you mean no? I've been slowly clearing things from that back room for a year, and it still looks like a hoarder's paradise. I'm giving you the desk."

Patrea shook her head. She'd let her hair grow longer over the past few months, so it swirled around her angular face in a soft, dark cloud. "It's worth far too much for you to just give it away. Let me buy it from you."

"I will not. You can consider it a gift or as payment for dealing with my legal woes. I don't care which, but I'm having David and Drew drop it off as soon as you're done painting." I gave her a smile. "Unless you wanted to keep using this folding table instead. I mean, it's only a little wobbly. Nothing a few matchbooks under the legs won't fix."

She grinned. "I feel like I should argue more, but I want the desk too much, so I'll just say thank you."

Setting my legal troubles on the back burner, I turned my attention toward being a good friend.

"You're doing okay with everything?" I ticked off the list of her most recent life changes. "The move, the new job. It's a lot all at once, but you look happy."

Visiting a place and living in it were not the same, and as much as I loved being back home in Mooselick River, I'd had to make some adjustments. But at least I'd known what I was getting into before I decided to come back. Patrea was about to get a crash course in small-town living, complete with nosy neighbors who had more imagination than common sense and a serious case of wagging tongues.

"I am," she said with enough conviction I had to believe her. "If you'd have asked me a year ago, I would have said I had everything I needed in life. I didn't know any better then, but now I do, and I have you to thank for it. You're like my fairy godmother."

Cursed with pale skin to go along with my red hair, I blush a lot. Even when there's nothing to blush about.

"It was nothing," I insisted. "I barely got a chance to wave my wand at all, and I didn't even have to go looking for mice and pumpkins."

"No," Patrea laughed. "Only for Christmas trees."

"And the hunky men who sell them."

In a few short weeks, Patrea would marry Chris Evergreen, the appropriately-named owner of the local Christmas tree farm. Tall, built, and opinionated, he made a perfect, if unlikely, match for the driven attorney.

"You know," I said, "Half the single women in town already hate you for taking that fine man off the market."

"Too bad for them, I guess. They can all come to the wedding and eat from the bitter fruit of jealousy."

"So, it's a vegan reception?" I teased.

She offered a rude hand gesture. "Fruitarian, actually. Speaking of which, I need to drop off a deposit check for the caterer today."

"Ooh, I'll go with you. I want to see the look on Mabel's face when you tell her what's on the menu."

Patrea's face changed. "I didn't hire Mabel." She noted the mild shock that sent my eyebrows arching. "I mean, her food is perfectly fine, but it's a little...provincial for a wedding. Not that I'm looking for anything pretentious, mind you."

I wanted to come to Mabel's defense, but since the local diner owner garnished most of her dishes with a sprig of curly kale and a wedge of orange or lemon, I supposed Patrea had a point. Worse, ever since my friend Jacy had given up being a waitress in favor of becoming a business owner, the service at the diner hadn't been quite as cheerful or efficient.

"Far be it from me to offer unwanted advice." I ignored her blatant snort of disagreement, "but if you want to make nice with the locals, it's probably good if you don't tick them off right during the wedding by hiring in an outsider."

"For your information, I did hire someone local. It just wasn't Mabel."

"You hired Summer Merryfield," I said, dismayed.

"I did. Why?" Patrea slid off her glasses, used the corner of her blouse to polish one lens. "What's wrong with Summer?"

"Nothing, really." I set my own loyalties aside. "As far as I know, she's a perfectly nice person, and I haven't heard anything negative about her cooking."

"But you've never tried her food?"

"Sorry," I had to admit. "I haven't. Summer only just opened up her little café this spring, and she keeps odd hours, so I keep forgetting to go."

"That's fair," Patrea said. "From what she told me, she's running on an alternative business model aimed at providing customers a more personal touch. She basically only serves brunch at the café during the week, and she's set up for catering, but I'm a little hazy on the rest."

"We'll ask her about it," I said. "Now, I'm intrigued."

"Good, then you can give me an unbiased opinion since I've gone ahead and scheduled a tasting party with her for tomorrow for Friday girl's night."

Surprised, I said, "What about Chris? Shouldn't the groom be the one to help decide on the menu?"

She waved the question away. "Please. Chris thought we should let the town throw us a potluck supper. Can you just imagine? Paper plates, paper napkins, and plastic utensils."

Not to mention a mostly bean-based menu—the go-to supper option for any town function.

"So, he doesn't get to choose, I take it?" I couldn't hold back a smile.

"No, he does not. I've given in on him wanting to invite practically the entire town on top of having his entire family coming in from all corners of the world. I went to the benefit dinner for the Morrison's, and I draw the line at my wedding reception turning into a fart-off."

I clamped down on my tongue and banished the mental image evoked by her choice of words. "I can see you've given this a lot of thought." Besides, Chris wouldn't care about the fussy details. He was more of a bottom-line kind of guy.

"Besides," Patrea echoed my thoughts, "Chris doesn't care what we eat as long as we're married when the day ends. He says all he wants is me." She sounded surprised, but then, up until Chris swept her off her feet, Patrea hadn't been able to see herself as deserving of love or happiness. Not one of her more endearing traits and one I was glad enough to see her growing away from. "So, it's a date for tomorrow? You'll tell Jacy and Neena about the venue change?"

"Sure. Maybe Paul's shark will get the case dropped by then, and I can celebrate my good fortune with semi-pretentious food." I knew I probably jinxed myself, but I said it anyway.

Chapter Two

Summer's place, Merry Eats, occupied the corner space of the old brick building that had housed Barron's Drug and Variety until a newer chain came in and knocked them out of business when I was still in grade school. Barron's had carried a little bit of everything behind the large, oak and glass double doors set diagonally into the building's front corner.

I couldn't walk past without being hit with fond memories of Grammie Dupree making a beeline for the glass case of hot nuts sitting at the end of the soda fountain counter. Cashews were her favorites, and I'd made them mine as well. All these years later, I still remembered the oily scent and the warm feel of them through the paper bag. And the way we'd munch on them while we wandered the aisles checking for new and interesting items.

After the store closed, the owners turned the upstairs into a pair of one-bedroom apartments and remodeled the downstairs into two retail spaces. Over the years, various businesses had gone in and out. Now, Summer's catering and lunch-only café took up the larger of the two, while the other sat empty.

"I heard there's a used bookstore coming in here next month," Jacy said.

"Are you sure," Neena countered. "I heard it was supposed to be a yarn or fabric store. Something crafty. Candles, maybe."

"No, I'm pretty sure it's books."

"Quit bickering." As instructed, Patrea rapped on the glass and waited. "I want your honest opinions," she said. "Don't hold back, okay? This is my wedding we're talking about, and I'm only doing this once, so it needs to be perfect." She peered through the wavy glass, looking for signs of Summer.

Jacy grinned. "Have you met us?"

"I have," Patrea turned to present a cocked eyebrow and a wry tone. "Miss Merry Sunshine spreading love and flowers wherever she goes, wouldn't say boo to a goose. I need you to say boo if there's a goose."

"Goose is really more suitable for a Christmas wedding, and I'd take that as an insult if I didn't love you so much." Jacy remained unflappable in the face of Patrea's wedding jitters and was saved from further discourse when Summer unlocked the door.

If I had to describe Summer with one word, it would be medium—which is what she was in both height and build. Her hair—covered today by a printed bandanna that came halfway down her forehead and tied in the back—fell somewhere in the middle area between blond and brunette.

"I'm so sorry." Her face red from either kitchen heat or embarrassment, Summer pressed a hand to her heart. "I meant to call you because I've done something incredibly stupid. I scheduled your tasting and didn't notice I already had two Table at Home bookings for tonight. I don't know what I was thinking."

We followed her inside. After taking a short detour to the cash register, Summer approached Patrea, pressed a check into her hand. "I'm sure you won't want to hire me now that I've proved I can be a scatterbrain. Here's your deposit back, and again, I'm so sorry."

Out of reflex, Patrea accepted the check. From where I stood, I got a good look at her face. The expression she wore was one I'd seen before. It was her lecture face.

"First rule of business, never return a deposit check until you've exhausted all other options," she offered Summer a mild rebuke.

Summer frowned. "I don't understand."

"Can you do the tasting tomorrow?"

"Really? Yes. Of course, I can. Most people aren't big on giving second chances, but I'd sure appreciate one."

Call me crazy, but I got the impression Summer wasn't thinking only of customers when she said that.

Patrea turned. "Tomorrow okay with you?" The question was meant for all three of us. I nodded, but Jacy shook her head, and so did Neena.

"I'll have to pass. We're hosting dinner with Brian's parents, so I've got a full day of cooking and cleaning to get our place ready to pass muster."

Neena cocked a thumb at Jacy. "I'm in the same boat as her, except I don't have to do the cooking, so I'll be running the shop. Viola thinks the only thing I know how to make is black-eyed peas and collard greens." She grinned. "I have decided not to disabuse her of that notion since it gets me out of inviting her over more often than once a month."

"Okay, then. Make it a tasting for two, and whatever it is I smell right now should definitely be on the menu."

"What is that?" I sniffed the air. Behind Summer's somewhat cloying, floral perfume that made me think of my grandmother, I picked up a familiar note. "Rhubarb?"

I knew I'd nailed it when Summer clapped her hands. "Yes," she said enthusiastically. "We've had an excellent crop this year and a longer growing season than normal. For one of tonight's desserts, I'm making custard with rhubarb compote. You see, I try to use seasonal and locally sourced ingredients whenever I can."

Summer inhaled. "I've added angelica stem to cut some of the rhubarb's tartness. It brings a slightly flowery note and an earthy flavor to the compote. Goes great with fish, too, so the two dishes complement each other nicely."

"Angelica? I'm not sure I've ever heard of that," I said.

"It's a lovely herb that grows wild around here if you know where to look."

While she seemed to enjoy her short, culinary lecture, Summer had glanced toward the kitchen twice while talking about the food. "I need to…" She nodded her head in that direction. "Come on."

Over her shoulder, she said, "I'm planning to offer cooking classes here in the fall."

"Sign me up," Neena said.

While she chopped and diced, Summer spoke passionately about her approach to cooking.

"Okay, sign me up, too. I'm hooked." I said as I watched Summer pull the top off a frost-coated plastic tub with *Lemon Sorbet* written in permanent marker on the lid. The sharp tang of citrus perfumed the air.

She selected a brown vial of extract from a drawer, shook a few drops into the sorbet, stirred, then tasted.

"Angelica again," she said as she put the dirty spoon in the sink. "In essence form. I'm using this one seasoning as the theme for an entire meal. It enhances the flavor of the lemons and reduces any bitterness." The sorbet went into the freezer, presumably to harden back up. "Just lucky I had a container in my freezer at home. It was a direct request, and I'd run out of stock here."

Someone banged on the back door to the kitchen and yelled, "Hey, let me in."

"Do you think you could get that for me?" Summer said.

Since Jacy was closest, she said, "Sure," and opened the door to admit Thea Lombardi. Mabel's waitress at the Blue Moon carried a metal stockpot between hands covered with oven mitts.

"This is hot." She cast an annoyed glare toward Summer, then stomped over and set the pot on the sink's metal drainboard with a clang. "Don't offer to help or nothing." She turned and headed back for the door, muttering the whole time about not having time to play errand girl and not even getting a tip.

No one spoke for a moment after the door slammed behind her, then Summer calmly went to the cooler, pulled out a tray with two metal pans on it. She retrieved the offending pot from where Thea had left it, opened the lid, and began to spoon fluffy mashed potatoes on top of the contents of one of the metal pans.

"Is that shepherd's pie?" Jacy craned her neck to see what was in the pans.

"An updated version made with braised sirloin tips and asparagus smothered in a caramelized onion and bacon jam." She smoothed out the potatoes with practiced hands, drizzled a little melted butter over them, and set the pans in the oven to finish off. Once the door shut behind them, she let out a satisfied sigh.

"Can that be on the tasting menu?" Patrea wanted to know.

Summer grinned. "It can be if you're not overly concerned with cost. Sirloin tips are a little pricier than the standard chicken or fish."

"Totally worth it," Patrea said. "As long it tastes as good as it smells."

Summer grinned again. "Would you consider it boastful if I said it's even better?"

"We'll get out of your hair, now." I grabbed Patrea's arm and eased her toward the door. "We've distracted you long enough."

But Patrea had one more question. "What's Table at Home?"

"It's my version of an elevated menu and personalized service," Summer said. "For those special evenings when you don't want to cook a fancy meal, but you want it to look like you did."

"You mean it's like stealth catering?" Neena asked, probably thinking how much fun it would be to give her mother-in-law a culinary surprise. Viola Montayne could be a handful and hadn't taken the death of her only son well—not that anyone could blame her for that. Neena had borne the brunt of Viola's grief for six months before forming a truce. Their relationship was better, but Neena still walked on eggshells at times.

Seeming delighted, Summer nodded. "Exactly. I deliver everything in oven-proof, disposable containers, so all you have to do is keep them warm until you're ready to eat, then slap the finished product on a serving plate. I even supply the garnish and dessert."

"I might have to remember that for after the honeymoon," Patrea said.

"You won't be disappointed. I also offer a less stealthy option that falls somewhere between catering and providing a cooking class from the comfort of a client's home."

"You'll just come to my house and cook? And I can watch?" Neena said.

"Sure. And you don't have to just watch. You can help. There's a brochure with a menu of options on that table by the door," Summer pointed. To Patrea, she said. "Come back tomorrow. I promise I'll knock your socks off."

"It's a date," Patrea passed the check back to her. "You keep this."

Summer pinned the check to the cooler door with a magnet as we headed for the door. Outside, I linked my arm around Patrea's. "While I wouldn't prefer it for your wedding supper, I'm prepared to eat a generous helping of crow. If her food tastes half as good as it looks and smells, we're in for a treat."

"It does," she assured. "And I won't have her put the black bird on the menu, but I will say I told you so."

"After all she's been through, I think it's a grand idea to give that poor woman some business. I know her a little since she's friendly with my mother—they get together and talk a lot about herbs and gardening and whatnot," Jacy chimed in. "Summer's always been a good cook, so when her husband dumped her a few months back, she decided to fall back on her best skill. She's not, like, classically trained or anything, but she likes to experiment, and from what my mom says, has a natural knack for combining flavors."

"Her husband left her? That's sad." I felt bad for Summer. Having your marriage implode was something I knew a little bit about. "Any idea what happened?" And I'd been avoiding her place out of loyalty to Mabel. I guess that made me a jerk.

"Not really."

"Do you think our regular table will still be open at Cappy's?" Neena wanted to know. She tucked a few dark curls behind one ear. "I don't know about y'all, but after that, I'm starvin'."

Chapter Three

For a Friday night, Cappy's was hopping.

A trick of the landscape hid the sprawling length of the local bar and grill so that from the front, Cappy's looked a whole lot smaller than it was. With live music—mostly country or rockabilly, the bar did a brisk business most every weekend.

"Place is packed tonight," I said to Miranda Perkins when she arrived at not our regular table with a pitcher of draft and a bottle of passable red wine—our standard Friday night order. Too late by far, we'd ended up stuck at a table in the corner near a low stage where the band would swing into action around nine.

Miranda's face looked flushed. "Midnight Highway's playing this week. They draw people in from out of town. Great for business, not so great for my feet." Knowing our preference, she dropped a basket with both rolls and mini bread loaves on the table, then pulled an ordering pad from her apron pocket. "If you know what you want, it's probably better to tell me now." She tilted her head to the left. "I got a birthday party over there that's taking up two tables. Kid just turned twenty-one, so

I'm expecting a long night. You order now, you can slide in ahead of them, but if you're not ready, I can come back."

"We'll order now," Neena's tone dared the rest of us to disagree. No one did.

We went for the appetizer sampler, a platter of wings for the table, and just to make it look like we weren't total junk food hounds—side salads all around.

"And darlin'," Neena said. "My belly's trying to eat my backbone, so you just go ahead and tell Milo to send things out whenever they're ready, okay?" The ordering done, she selected a mini honey wheat loaf, broke it in half, and slathered the fragrant bread with butter.

Our regular table sat on a raised section up near the bar where the noise level wasn't nearly as high as our present one. To our left, banquet seating lined the wall leading toward the door. A wagon wheel converted into a light fixture barely lit each table, making for an intimate atmosphere. Wall-mounted jukebox controllers took away from the romantic feel, but for Mooselick River, the corner booths were as good as it got. Many a new relationship began in one of them. More than a few ended there, too.

"When I turned down the potluck wedding supper and reception in the gym at the high school, Chris suggested we have it here. Can you just imagine?" Patrea tipped up the pitcher to fill her glass.

"I had my reception here," Jacy said in a mild tone. "No one seemed to mind." Her level look got her point across well enough to turn Patrea's face an embarrassed red.

"I'm sorry. That came out way snobbier than I meant it to sound."

Jacy's eyebrow arched. "Really? How snobby did you mean it to sound?"

I exchanged a glance with Neena. Jacy's temper burned the same way she drove: hot, fast, and with a certain dramatic flair. She never stayed mad long, but it was ugly while it lasted. This would be Patrea's first experience with it, and I doubted she'd done herself any favors with her Merry Sunshine crack earlier.

Frustrated, Patrea loosely curled her fingers, pressed the palm of her hand just above the outer corner of her eyebrow as if there might be a headache stirring there. "Listen, my family will have certain expectations."

Jacy's mouth opened, but Patrea cut her off. "Which doesn't make them snobs. It just means they're used to such events being held in less rustic surroundings. And before you get all worked up, I turned down their offer to pay for the whole thing if we had it at the Ballantine." Patrea named the ritziest hotel within a hundred miles. One with a gorgeous, Art Deco-style ballroom where I'd put on several gala functions in the past.

"La-ti-da," Jacy deadpanned.

"I turned them down," Patrea said, "because I want to get married here in Mooselick River, where Chris has family. Where we're going to make our life. Where my friends forgive me when I'm too blunt and where I finally feel like I've come home."

"You make it really difficult," Jacy let a tiny smile play across her lips, "to stay mad at you."

"What have you got planned so far?" Neena asked.

"We're having the whole thing at the farm." Patrea paused while Miranda delivered our salads, then doused hers with house dressing. "I agreed to have the ceremony among the Christmas trees, but I drew the line at going all out with the seasonal theme. She speared a cherry tomato and waved it around as she talked.

"Christmas in July? I can see why you'd want to avoid that," Jacy said, all trace of her mild annoyance a thing of the past.

Except the notion gave me ideas. "I think there's a middle ground in there somewhere. Chris sells potted trees, right?" I asked.

Patrea nodded. "Sure. Every year, people grow more eco-conscious, which means the market for live trees is trending up. Chris decided he was leaving money on the table if he didn't at least try to meet the need." Look at her, making all kinds of business sense.

"Have you thought about setting up the ceremony on the side lawn? There's plenty of room and a decent view, besides. I'm picturing a variety of potted firs in elegant, white pots arranged behind and around the altar. Then maybe use some smaller pots as a border around the seating to make everything feel more intimate."

"Okay, I see where you're going with this." Jacy selected a wing from the platter almost before it settled fully on the table. "A white carpet running down the aisle between two banks of rental chairs—the white kind to keep everything crisp and clean. Fir trees in all the shades of green spearing out of elegant white pots and covered in twinkle lights. It could work."

"It does sound nice," Patrea allowed. "Pays tribute to the family business but doesn't cross the line into territory that would make my folks uncomfortable."

"Have you decided on dress colors for the bridesmaids?" Nearly choking on a hasty bite of lettuce, Neena's question came out somewhat garbled.

"Not red." Patrea's tone was as dry as the wine she'd switched to with her meal. "On top of the obvious holiday connotations, I'd rather not send my mother to an early grave over a choice she'd deem vulgar."

A second too late, Patrea glanced at Jacy to see the annoyance back on her face. "Don't tell me, your attendants wore red."

"Well, burgundy, because the brighter shades aren't flattering to Everly's skin tones, and, unlike some brides, I wanted my entire wedding party to shine," Jacy said.

"I guess I should have just ordered fried shoe for dinner since I'm spending so much time with my foot in my mouth," Patrea said. "I didn't mean to hurt your feelings. I'm sorry." She reached over to lay her hand on Jacy's. "I'm sure your wedding was tasteful and lovely."

Relenting, Jacy smirked. "Tasteful? No. Not according to your standards, but it was loud and fun, and everyone had a great time."

"Cerulean." Having sucked the last of the meat off a spicy chicken wing, Neena tossed the bones on the platter and the color choice into the mix. "It's a pretty shade that will work for all of us. The blue tones will bring out Jacy's eyes, but it also has enough green to go perfectly with Everly's hair, and I look good in everything."

Without waiting for confirmation, Neena selected another wing. "That's colors and the basics of the ceremony. Let's talk reception. Band or deejay?"

Her matter-of-fact tone triggered an arch look from Patrea, but the bride-to-be offered no contradiction. Was this the same Patrea who could tell the difference between three virtually identical colors of gray? It seemed it was because she calmly let someone else choose her wedding colors.

"We could rent one of those big party tents with the dance floor." Despite my misgivings, Patrea seemed to be getting into the spirit of the planning. "Decorate the inside with more potted trees to keep with the theme. String up scads of fairy lights, and I'd say we're good to go. Simple enough to keep Chris from feeling out of place, but elegant enough my mother won't have a conniption."

"Are you sure about that? A party tent on a Christmas tree farm is not the Ballantine," Jacy pointed out. Maybe she hadn't entirely let go of her pique.

"I'm sorry to butt in." I hadn't even noticed the couple at the next table, but apparently, the woman had noticed us. "But I've been eavesdropping, which is terribly rude, I know. I just couldn't help myself. You see, I'm getting married in the fall, and…"

Tall with hair nearly the same color as mine, I recognized her only as a hairdresser in the salon where my mother got her hair done. Twisting in her seat, she reached for the bag hanging on the back of her chair, withdrew one of those thick, organizer notebooks.

After a word with whoever else was at her table—I couldn't see past Neena without shifting in my seat—she rose and came to stand over ours.

"I have my planning book with me." Without asking, she shoved platters and plates of our food aside to make space and flipped open the cover. "I have everything organized and color-coded, see? This is my dress."

For the life of me, I couldn't dredge up the woman's name, or maybe I'd never heard it. Not that much older than me, we'd have gone to school together if she'd been born and raised here. We hadn't, so I figured she was a newer transplant in town. I would have introduced myself and asked for her name, but the woman never stopped talking long enough for me to get a word in.

She selected a tab, used it to flip the book open to the desired page giving us a good, long look at the photo of the dress she'd chosen. Elegant and understated were not words I would use to describe it. Ugly wasn't the right word, either, because someone took the time and effort to create the explosion of tulle and lace, and I wouldn't want to disparage the effort they put in. Fluffy. That was a good word to use. Or maybe ruffled was closer. Bell-like was another. Wide. It was a lot of dress. A whole lot.

"That's..." Jacy's search for the right word made the woman smile.

"It is," she said. "Isn't it? Looks like it belongs on a Barbie doll in a pretty pink box." She flipped a few more pages to show us photos of her bridesmaid dresses, and then the venue—the new resort in Hackinaw, the one that had sparked a redesign of the road system so it bypassed Mooselick River and nearly ruined our economy. Figured.

"It looks nice," I said, hoping she'd close up her book and leave. Patrea's fingers tapped on the table, a sure sign of increasing annoyance. "I'm sure you'll have a wonderful day."

"We're going with the gold-level package because it's the best value. I'll get a full spa treatment on the morning of the wedding, plus the works at their in-house salon for the entire wedding party. Really, they take care of everything. All you have to do is pick out the dress and show up. If you like, I'll give you a referral. It's good for a five percent discount on all but the platinum package."

"Well, I——" Patrea started to say something, but the table-hopping bride-to-be cut her off.

"If you refer three bookings, they'll upgrade you to the platinum package for free." Whatshername pulled out a brochure, laid it alongside Patrea's plate, then closed up her planner. "You really should take the tour, at least. The facilities are top-notch."

At that point, I think Patrea would have agreed to almost anything to get her to go away. "I'll do that."

We all watched the bride-to-be go back to her table, Jacy's eyes widening when she got a look at the man seated there.

"Summer's ex," Jacy mouthed, and so, of course, we all had to take a look. We were not discreet about it, either, though he didn't notice our scrutiny as he was too wrapped up in his tablemate. Still, we had to wait until they left before Jacy could give us the scoop.

"Okay," she said as soon as the coast was clear. "I'm assuming by the blank looks none of you get your hair done at Do or Dye. That was Peggy Sullivan. I knew Jack Merryfield and Summer split up, but I had no idea he'd taken up with Peggy. And they're already talking wedding, so you know what that means."

I followed her train of thought. "Jack moves fast, or else they'd been carrying on for a while before Summer found out."

"Or it's the other thing," Neena pointed out. "And they're trying to get married before she starts showing."

"Only time will tell," Jacy said. "Now, where were we?"

"Looks like girl's night is over." Patrea gestured toward the bar's entrance with her wine glass.

I glanced over to see Jacy's husband, Brian standing near the end of the bar, looking toward our regular table. With him were my boyfriend, Drew Parker, Patrea's Chris, and our friend, David Barrington.

"Over here," Jacy popped up from her seat and did that thumb and index finger whistle she'd tried to teach me for years. I still had no idea how it worked, but it certainly got Brian's attention.

"Mind if we crash the party?" The first to arrive at our table, Brian leaned down to give Jacy a kiss. "My mom came by and picked up the baby about an hour ago, and we haven't had a night out in a while, so…here I am."

"And you brought reinforcements." I put my hand over Drew's since he'd circled around and rested both of his on my shoulders.

"Safety in numbers." Brian's grin lit up his whole face. He hadn't been too worried about Jacy's response. Ten years in, the childhood sweethearts still only had eyes for one another. You couldn't look at them without feeling warm and fuzzy inside. "I didn't expect the place to be packed like this, though."

The only empty table was a two-top near the bar. "If you and Jacy want to turn this into date night, you'd better grab that table before it's gone."

"Trying to get rid of me?" Jacy smiled but wasted no time vacating her chair. "I see how you are."

"Go. You're no good to us now, anyway. Not once you have your hot husband on the brain." Making Brian blush was almost a sport. Any compliment will do it, and it's fun. Mention his butt, and he loses the ability to speak.

"I'll grab a couple of folding chairs from the back," Chris brushed a hand over Patrea's hair as he walked past. "I know where they are."

David settled into the chair Jacy left behind, which put him on my left with Neena on his. More comfortable now with being in a room full of people, he picked up a cold onion ring from her plate. "You mind?" he asked.

Neena shook her head, nudged her plate closer just as the band took the stage for their first number.

By unspoken agreement, Chris and Patrea hit the dance floor. We watched them for a moment because the way they moved, it was hard not to.

29

"No reason they should have all the fun." To my surprise, David turned to Neena, cocked his head toward the floor. "You wanna?"

She flashed me a glance, then shrugged. "Why not?"

The band's first set passed in a blur of dancing and nibbling from the second sampler the men ordered, and we were all on the floor when the lead singer announced they'd do a slow song and then take a break.

In a move worthy of Fred Astaire, David swung Neena in close, cradled her against him, and swayed to the slow throb of a love song. I watched over Drew's shoulder, saw the lightning strike David when Neena closed her eyes and rested her cheek against his shoulder.

Chapter Four

"That's weird." On Saturday, Patrea knocked on the door of Merry Eats for the third time, then cupped her eyes with her palms, pressing the sides of her hands against the window to block out enough light for a decent look through the textured glass. "I don't smell anything cooking, and I don't hear anyone moving around in there. She wouldn't flake on me again, right?"

She tried the door, and it opened. We exchanged a look before stepping over the threshold. The familiar sinking sensation in my stomach and the dead silence boded ill.

Patrea beat me to the door, took one look, and backed away. I already had my phone in my hand when I walked past her. "We're too late," I said, needlessly. Face gray, eyes wide and staring, her head lying in a pool of vomit—that Summer was gone was painfully obvious. That her death hadn't been an easy one, even more so. A wave of sympathy overwhelmed me—what a sad waste of a life.

Carol Ann Wilmette answered the emergency call. Why was she always on duty whenever I found a dead body? And yes, I am aware that the larger question should have been, why was I *always* finding corpses, but at this point, I'd decided to stop asking that one.

"911, what's your emergency?" Carol Ann asked again.

"Uh, it's Everly Dupree."

"Who's dead now?"

"Why do you assume someone's dead every time I call?"

I heard the pop of a gum bubble. "So someone's not dead? What's your emergency, then?"

I sighed. "No, someone is."

There was an expectant silence on the other end of the phone, then the bubble sound again. "You gonna tell me, or do I have to guess?"

"It's Summer Merryfield. You'd better send Ernie over to the café right away."

"You want me to stay on the line until he gets there?"

Carol must have had some new training because she'd never asked me that before. "No, I know the drill. Don't touch anything, don't move the body. Just send him over." I tapped the end button and put my phone away.

Patrea lurched toward the small table near the door, put her hands down on it to steady herself, then pulled out one of the chairs and sat. She looked at me much the same as I suspected Carol would have if I'd walked into the station. I don't mind saying it hurt a little.

"I didn't do anything," I defended myself. "Don't look at me like I'm the harbinger of death. It's not my fault if I keep ending up in the wrong place at the wrong time."

"How awful is it that my first thought was there goes the food for my wedding?" Patrea pressed two fingers in the spot between her eyebrows. "I'm a selfish, horrible person."

Taking care to stay back from the body, I reassured Patrea while trying to take in as many details as possible just in case Summer's death hadn't been accidental.

"Of course, you're not. We all have those weird reflex thoughts when confronted with death. It's only natural." I skirted the steel-topped table where Summer had been working, made my way to the stove, grabbed a set of tongs from a nearby container, and used them to lift the lid of a pot and look at its cold, congealed contents.

"You're not supposed to touch anything, remember?" Patrea's voice sounded tired.

"I didn't touch the stove." My voice sounded defensive.

"You touched the tongs."

So I had, I thought, dismayed. And since it was too late to go back and undo what I had done, I used them to open one of the oven doors letting out a waft of the scent of something sweet. The smell came from a baking sheet containing a single layer of pale, green stalks sliced at an angle that made them look like a bit like pasta and coated in sugar that looked to have gone damp and sticky.

The second oven held a pan of herb-studded chicken that looked about half cooked. I nudged the door shut with my knee. Both ovens had been turned off before the food had time to finish cooking.

"I'll fess up when Ernie gets here. And you touched the chair and the table." I didn't tack on a *so there*, but my tone did.

I circled the body looking for signs of foul play but saw nothing obvious. Summer lay on her side, her body curved inward. I couldn't see or smell blood, but that could have been masked by the smell of vomit.

"Looks like Summer ate something that disagreed with her."

With no telltale chill in the air, no chatty ghost hovering, either, I assumed we hadn't disturbed an active crime scene and said as much to Patrea.

"I'll be the judge of that," Ernie hadn't made any noise as he entered the café, probably because we'd left the door open behind us. "What did you touch, Everly?"

As succinctly as possible, I told Ernie what I'd done. As he knelt to examine Summer's body, I explained how we'd come to find her lying on her kitchen floor. Patrea pitched in to back me up. The story didn't take long to tell, and by the time it was done, the ambulance had pulled up out front.

"That's it," I said. "I met the woman for the first time yesterday, and now she's gone. It's sad, really." I stepped back to let the medics bring in their equipment, recognizing the first man through the door.

Vinnie De Luca was here in both his current positions. I suspected he'd been elected to be the county's coroner because he had at least some medical training, and no one else wanted the job. Maybe if we lived in a larger area, the poor man could have given up his paramedic shifts and spent his days just wearing one hat...or would that be one lab coat? I'd heard through the grapevine—in the form of Martha Tipton—that Vinnie had applied to work for the state medical examiner in some capacity. According to Martha, Vinnie had aspirations—she'd wrinkled her nose over the word—that involved moving to Augusta.

"Poison," he said after a quick examination. "Would be my first guess. Accidental, most likely. We'll have to send her to Augusta for an autopsy. The lab techs will have to run a tox screen to be certain." He stood and scanned the items scattered across the tall, steel-topped table where Summer had been slicing and dicing ingredients. "It'll take time for the results to come back."

"Any way you can get the ME to put a rush on it?" Ernie said.

"I've got some pull, but probably not enough to move us to the front of the line for what's clearly death by misadventure. I'll do what I can, though."

While he talked, Vinnie picked up samples of the chopped vegetables, dropped them in small plastic bags, and set them aside. He did the same with the contents of a lidless, plastic container that looked like the one we'd seen with the sorbet. Next, he went over to the stockpot, sniffed the contents, then took a small sample of that and another from the contents of the tray in the oven.

Part of Vinnie's job was to look at the evidence and decide the cause of death, but that pronouncement generally came after the autopsy. If Ernie suspected homicide, he could call the state police and a tech team to investigate the crime. Since he was on the spot, and because he leaned toward an accidental poisoning, it looked like Vinnie had decided to take on the job all by himself.

"Shouldn't you call in someone more official to do that?"

Ernie glared at me when I asked, but Vinnie answered before Ernie had a chance to tell me to mind my business.

"I'm this close," he held up his thumb and index finger with less than half an inch between them, "to finishing my degree in forensics. I think I'm capable of collecting evidence," he said in a how-dare-you-question-me tone.

A tall, square trash can lined with a black plastic bag sat at the end of Summer's worktable. As Vinnie passed by the can, he glanced down, then stopped short, and looked harder. Whatever he saw there sent his eyebrows upward and had him reaching into one of his pockets for a pair of rubber gloves, which he put on with practiced movements.

"Find something?" Ernie's shoes squeaked on the tile as he walked over to take a look for himself. He reached down, possibly to tilt the can toward better lighting, but Vinnie swatted Ernie's hand away before it made contact.

"Don't touch that with your bare hands, you fool."

Ernie's face flushed a dull red at being called a fool, but he kept his cool. Another reason why I maintain Ernie is a good cop.

"That's Cicuta maculata. Commonly known as water hemlock. Every part of the plant is poisonous. We'll need to send a sample to the lab to be certain, but this is gonna be your cause of death. I'll stake my reputation and stand you a week's pay if I'm wrong."

Too cool to flinch, Ernie slowly and deliberately shoved his hand in his pocket, rocked up on his toes to get a look at the offending plant matter. "You sure? Looks like Queen Anne's lace from here."

"I'm sure. The diameter of the stems is a dead giveaway."

Vinnie's poor choice of term earned him a sidelong look from Patrea, but by unspoken agreement, we'd stayed quiet during the past few minutes. Call me nosy, but I didn't want Ernie kicking us out until we'd heard everything there was to hear.

"Something like this happens every year or two in Maine. You get your amateur botanists who insist on foraging for mushrooms and other edibles, and they're never careful enough. Mistake destroying angel mushrooms for white caps or hemlock for angelica, and instead of a nicely seasoned meal, they're serving up a plateful of death."

I heard Patrea suck in a breath at about the same time I realized that, had Summer not taste-tested her own dish, we'd have been tucking into that plateful of death right about now. All the blood drained out of my face leaving it, I was sure, paler than it naturally was, which was saying something. Intense emotions washed over me— fear, relief, sorrow—leaving a chill in their wake. I shivered. Beside me, Patrea did the same and clasped her hands together to stop them from shaking.

It wasn't my first brush with death, but this time things were different. The danger hadn't come at me from the front in an all-out assault but sneaked up from behind.

This time, I didn't have any sort of adrenaline rush to carry me along, so the impact hit harder.

"I suppose she's better off this way." Ernie watched the paramedics put on extra protection before attending to the body. "If she'd have opened up for lunch, no telling how many people she'd have killed."

"The hell I would." Summer's voice came from behind me and turned my veins to icy streams. I closed my eyes slowly and hoped that when I opened them again, it would be to wake up from a bad dream.

A doomed wish, of course.

"Condescending jackass. Who does he think he is?" Summer ranted. "My grandmother taught me more than he'll ever know about wild edibles. I'm not some idiot wandering the woods with a guidebook and no clue. I have eyes, don't I? And a nose. And more than half a brain, too."

With every syllable she uttered, Summer's ear-popping energy rose higher. I felt the prickle across the back of my neck, the buzzing in my throat, the tiny hairs standing up along my arms. Surrounded by people who clearly weren't able to sense the disturbance—though I did see a shudder run through Patrea's body, and she had once mentioned feeling a presence in my house—I couldn't turn and tell Summer to shut up. I dearly wanted to, mind you, but not as much as I wanted to avoid giving

Ernie one more reason to look at me funny. So, I kept quiet and let her run down.

"I've been cooking with angelica for years. I've never poisoned anyone before, and I certainly wouldn't be stupid enough to cut up hemlock with my bare hands. Do you see any gloves laying around here, genius?"

Summer waved her finger under the ME's nose. "Do you? And look at my hands. Are there contact burns on them? No, there are not, and there would be if I were stupid enough to handle hemlock without protection. How did you get that job anyway?"

Vinnie didn't even flinch when she put her face close to his. I did, though. Maybe other people can't feel anything, but being that close to a ghost isn't a pleasant experience for me. The nearest real-life experience I can compare it to is walking barefooted through ankle-deep muck. Touching a ghost is like that, only over my entire body, and the muck is icy cold besides.

The thing that finally shut Summer up was the sound of the zipper closing on the body bag. Maybe she hadn't fully realized she was dead until then, but she quit talking right in the middle of a sentence and seemed to become more aware of her surroundings. I watched from the sidelines hoping she wouldn't notice I could see her.

Would I feel lousy if she didn't know there was someone in the living world who might help her find justice should there come the need? Probably, but I figured I could live with the guilt if it meant her not following me home and bugging me until I did.

Mooselick River is the kind of small town where people will follow an ambulance or fire truck out of morbid curiosity. Plus, Carol Ann Wilmette has a big mouth. Whether she called Summer's ex, or some other lookie-loo did, the result was the same because he picked that moment to show up and shove his way past the pair of deputies Ernie had called in to help.

"Summer?" Jack Merryfield stumbled to a halt at the sight of the black body bag being loaded onto a gurney for transport. "It can't be." Frantic, he searched the room for someone who might tell him what had happened. When his gaze fell on Patrea and me, he frowned, then latched onto Ernie as the best possible source of information.

"What happened? I heard...tell me that's not Summer." He moved closer to the gurney, and I think he would have gone for the zipper if Ernie hadn't stepped in front of him.

"Don't!" Given in a gentler tone than I'd have expected, the command still stopped Jack from following through on his quest for assurance that Summer was dead. "Let Vinnie take care of her now."

"I don't understand." Breathing heavy, Jack grabbed the front of Ernie's shirt. "Tell me what happened."

For an ex-husband, the man took distraught to a new level. Watching him melt down put my response to the situation into perspective, calmed my anxiety a notch or two. Patrea's, too, I guessed when I caught her expression.

And then, I made my fatal mistake. I looked over at Summer to see what she might be thinking, and she caught me. Her eyes widened as she hovered nearby.

"You can see me."

Too late, I tried to let my gaze pass over her as if she weren't there, but it wasn't enough.

"You can see me." She said again with such relief I couldn't help myself. I looked at her deliberately, nodded my head slowly, then tried to communicate using subtle expressions that we couldn't talk with everyone around.

I wasn't looking forward to the moment when she got me alone because, in my experience, her presence could only mean one thing: murder.

Chapter Five

Given Summer's ghostly presence at my elbow, I probably needed to let Ernie know her death hadn't been accidental. There was a chance, I supposed, but my experience with spirits proved otherwise. Besides, she'd given me an excellent way to start the conversation. However, I waited until we were standing outside, watching the ambulance pull away with flashing lights but no sirens. Having pulled himself together enough to drive, Jack followed behind.

"Did you notice there weren't any red marks on her hands?" I think Ernie had forgotten we were there because his head swiveled around quickly when I spoke.

"Why are you still here?" he said, proving my theory.

I wasn't going to answer that. "I remember Grammie Dupree going out to get rid of some hemlock growing near that little marshy spot down by her place."

At the time, I'd found the getup she'd worn amusing—particularly given the heat of the day.

"She suited up for it. Pants tucked into her socks, yellow rubber gloves up to her elbows, a bandanna over her face, and a zip-up sweatshirt with the hood pulled so tight only her eyes showed. She said she wasn't taking any chances her bare skin would touch the plants because of the contact rash."

"So?"

"So." I held up mine. "Don't you think Summer would have a rash on her hands if she'd been out harvesting or accidentally cooking up a batch of hemlock?"

He gave me his quit-meddling look. I knew it well; this was not my first time seeing it. "Not if she wore gloves."

"Okay," I said, "but I didn't see any gloves, and if she wore them, wouldn't it mean she knew she was handling poison? And if she knew, do you think she'd be stupid enough to ingest it?"

Ernie's eyes narrowed. Above lips pressed into a firm line, his nostrils flared. He gets that same look on his face almost every time we speak. I refuse to take it personally. Just because I can see the recently murdered doesn't make me a dead body magnet. I don't think.

"Maybe you have a point. I'll wait for the ME's ruling, but it can't hurt to ask a few questions." He pulled the door shut behind him and indicated with a head nod that we should be on our way.

Not ten steps toward the car, Patrea spoke.

"I think you missed your calling." I realized she'd had hardly said a word during the whole ordeal, and now her tone was one I'd never heard her use before.

"What do you mean?"

"All that stuff about gloves and contact rashes," she said. "You think Summer was murdered."

I slid into the passenger's seat of Patrea's car and thought about my answer while she circled around to the other side and decided to keep it simple. "I do." And what's more, I found it interesting Ernie hadn't needed all that much convincing.

Patrea fitted the key into the ignition, then sat there for a moment, her head turned toward me, her eyes searching my face for something, but I wasn't sure what.

Finally, she said, "There's something you're not telling me."

"I don't know what you're talking about." If I kept the conversation going in circles, maybe she'd let it go.

She turned the key, glanced to see that the street was clear, then pulled out of the parking space. "You do." A moment passed, then she said, "Everyone's entitled to their secrets, but I hope you know you can trust me."

"I do." But I let the perfect moment pass. "I do trust you." It wasn't a lie. Trusting her wasn't the reason I held myself back, but thankfully, she didn't push.

"Someone murdered that poor woman, and if you hadn't been there, the whole thing would have been passed off as an accident."

"Oh, please!" I could all but hear Summer's eyes rolling as she sat in the back seat. "You didn't do anything except repeat everything I said to you."

"I know." I said it more for Summer's benefit than Patrea's. "But for what it's worth, I think Ernie was already leaning that way. I know what people say about him sometimes, but he's a good man, and a decent cop, too."

The worst thing I'd ever seen him do was let a pretty girl flirt her way out of a ticket once or twice.

"Maybe so." Not seeming convinced, Patrea quirked a brow, and when I chanced a glance at Summer, she wore the same expression.

Wisely, I chose not to belabor the point.

The morning after her death, Summer looked over my shoulder as I sprinkled chopped chives into my pan of scrambled eggs. "You should try fresh oregano next time. It has a nice bite to it, and It's good to mix things up once in a while."

The advice might be helpful; the chill of her presence was less so.

"You're getting too close again," I said, "and I don't have fresh oregano."

She stepped, or rather hovered, back. "Don't be ridiculous. That plant growing at the end of your back porch is oregano."

I stopped stirring the eggs and stared at her. "You mean the one with the pretty pink flowers? The one that spreads like crazy."

Summer nodded. "That's the one."

"Huh," I said, "I thought it was just a weed, but the bees love it, so I didn't have the heart to dig it up. Thanks, I'll give it a try next time."

When I turned to scoop eggs onto Drew's plate, I noticed his expression and realized I'd just carried on a one-sided conversation in front of him.

"I take it we're not alone." He kept his face turned toward me, his eyes flicking back and forth to see if he could make out the ghost.

"Summer's here. She was just telling me that we have oregano growing in the backyard and that it would make a welcome change from chives in our eggs." It felt like I'd begun to babble, but I couldn't seem to stop. "We have plenty of that growing out there, too."

I wouldn't call the look on Drew's face panic because that wouldn't be manly, but it lived in the same zip code. Having ghosts around probably seemed less creepy in the abstract, and now that he was staring down the reality, we'd see if he still wanted to move in together.

Ghosts showed up here occasionally. That was just a fact of my life these days. I didn't seek them out, I didn't want them here, and I didn't have any control over the situation. What I did have was a set of rules I asked my less-than-substantial guests to live by—or not live by, I supposed.

"Summer," I said firmly, "I really want to help you, but you do remember I said there were rules, don't you?"

She shrugged. "I thought they were more like guidelines."

My eggs were getting cold, and I needed more coffee if we were going to get into this in front of Drew. He hadn't touched his plate, either.

"Okay," I topped off my mug and squared off with Summer as much to reiterate the rules with her as to let Drew know what they were. "Let's go over this again. The first rule is: don't expect me to talk to you when there are other people around."

"Hey, you didn't have to answer, and you did say your man knows about your ghost problem, so I didn't think he counted."

I sighed because she had at least half of a good point. "Fine, then. I'll amend the rule. Don't talk to me at all unless I am alone, which brings us to the second rule. You need to respect my personal space. You don't show up in my bedroom or my bathroom. Ever." That one had been more for the male ghosts, but even so...there's such a thing as privacy.

Following only half the conversation, Drew cut in, "You didn't tell me there have been ghosts in the bedroom. I've been naked in there."

It was too early in the day for this.

"There have been no ghosts in the bedroom while you were naked." I was reasonably certain it was a fact.

It didn't help that Summer grinned and said, "Tempting, though. He certainly is pretty."

Or that I couldn't help but respond in kind. "Yes, he is."

"What? What am I?" Drew wanted to know.

"See, this is why I made the rule." I turned toward Summer. "Talking about him when he can't hear you is rude." To Drew, I said, "She thinks you're pretty."

"Oh." He went red in the face. You just have to love a man who's both hot and easily embarrassed when someone points it out. Or I do, anyway.

"And the third rule has to do with family contact. I don't do goodbye messages from beyond the grave, so don't even bother to ask." Not without a really good reason. They're my rules, I can break them if I want to, and I had broken this one on occasion.

"Listen, Ev. I think I'm going to head out for a run. You clearly need a moment here, and I'm just in the way."

Drew stood, leaned down, and gave me a peck on the cheek. "Back soon, okay?"

When he'd gone, I looked at Summer. "See what you did?"

She had the grace to look contrite as I scraped two plates of cold eggs into the trash and topped off my coffee mug for the third time.

"I'm sorry." Summer's tone clearly said the statement was a lie. "But I'm the injured party here. I'm the one who's dead. How about a little sympathy and understanding?"

I whirled on her, "You are an uninvited guest in my home. I'm sorry you're dead, and I've said I'd help you, but I don't owe you anything, so follow the rules or get out."

"Fine," she held up her hands in surrender. "I won't talk to you when Mr. Pretty is around."

"Thanks, and now that we're alone, how much can you tell me about what happened to you? Did anyone else come in after we left the café on Friday?"

"No, not then, and there's really not much to tell. I cooked, I packed up the meals, and I delivered them as planned. Then, I went back to clean up and do some of the prep for Patrea's tasting. I remember making a batch of candied angelica and putting some chicken in to roast. And then,"

What she would have said next got drowned out by the scrabble of toenails on hardwood when the doorbell rang, the sound of it sending my dog, Molly, tearing through the house.

"You should take that dog for some obedience training," Summer said. She didn't look happy when I made a derisive sound.

"Been there, done that. Took a pass on the T-shirt since it nearly got me killed."

Even through the wavy glass, I knew the silhouette of the man standing on my front porch. "Summer, you need to go. Now, please."

The ghost version of flouncing out of a room leaves a chill in the air and a somewhat ominous feeling behind but was preferable to her commentary on my cooking.

"Hey, Ernie. Want breakfast?" He stopped to give Molly a scratch behind the ears before following me to the kitchen, where I poured him the last of the coffee and put on a kettle for tea. I like both and had already passed my caffeine limit for the morning.

"Smells like you already ate," he said, but he didn't turn down the offer.

"You'd think, wouldn't you? But no, even though it wasn't for lack of trying."

"Huh?" I'd confused him.

"Never mind," I said. "What can I do for you? Besides breakfast, I mean."

"There's been a new development in the Merryfield case."

I dropped slices of bread into the toaster and waited for him to elaborate. When they'd finished browning, he still hadn't spoken. Not a good sign. Not a good sign at all.

"Tuck in," I set his plate of eggs and toast on the table, settled across from him, and began to eat while Ernie did the same. Whatever it was he didn't want to tell me could wait until my stomach wasn't churning with hunger. Apparently, he felt the same because he didn't speak until he'd finished.

"Frank Bodine died at about six o'clock yesterday morning." His fork clattered on the plate as he put it down. "And his wife is in the hospital with hemlock poisoning. Margo had to have her stomach pumped, and she's not completely out of the woods, but her prognosis is cautiously optimistic." Ernie made air quotes.

"Hemlock. Just like Summer."

"Exactly like Summer." Ernie drained his coffee. "Considering Summer cooked their supper."

I've seen Ernie put on the flat-eyed, authoritative expression before. He's pretty good at it when he wants to be. This time, he couldn't pull it off. Or else I was too stunned for it to register.

"You don't think she poisoned them on purpose? That's ridiculous." My jaw dropped.

"Vinnie's ready to declare the whole thing an accident based on the visual similarities between hemlock and wild angelica, but we have to wait for the toxicology reports to come back."

Shaking my head, I said, "Still hard to believe."

His expression shuttered. "It is."

"What aren't you telling me?"

"Vinnie has a theory. He thinks Frank's death was accidental, but he's leaning hard toward something else in Summer's case even without seeing the autopsy reports. The theory is that she realized her mistake and took a dose of hemlock out of remorse."

It didn't go down like that, or else Summer wouldn't be haunting me, but I couldn't say that to Ernie. All I could do was shake my head and reiterate that I didn't think she was that type of person.

"You never know what's in someone's heart. For all we know, Summer meant to murder the Bodines and then accidentally poisoned herself."

There was something in his tone that didn't fit what he said.

"But you don't believe that. Or that she realized her mistake and then committed suicide, do you?"

"The plants in her trash can were angelica." Not a no, but not yes, either. Still, it was good enough for me. "I called in a botanist from the extension office to confirm."

"Looks like Vinnie owes you a week's pay." A new thought popped into my head. "I forgot to tell you, she had two sets of what she called Table at Home meals that night. Was anyone else hurt?"

"No. Only the Bodines and Summer."

I already knew what I knew, but Ernie got there without a pesky ghost to lead the way. "You don't think her death was an accident. You think it was murder."

Ernie shrugged. "It feels too cut and dried, especially given the timing, but it doesn't matter what I believe. If the ruling comes down as either accidental or suicide, my hands are tied."

We'd finally come to the point of his visit.

"But mine aren't. Ernie Polk," I said in a grave tone. "Are you asking me to meddle?"

"No,"

Liar, I thought, and shouldn't have said out loud, but I did. "You're a big, fat liar. You don't just show up on my doorstep dropping information about a case without reason, and we both know it."

"Vinnie's convinced he knows what happened, the ME's office is so backlogged it's likely they'll do the autopsies but still accept his take on it, and the tox screens won't be back for weeks. I merely came to tell you which way the wind is blowing."

Rising to leave, Ernie kept his back to me, let his parting comment trail behind as he went out the door. "What you do with the information is up to you."

"Hey," I said, and he stopped in the act of turning the doorknob, "What was on the baking sheet in the oven?"

"Candied angelica."

The front door closed gently behind him, and I don't know how long I sat with a cold cup of tea in my hand, and my mind racing over the possibilities. Long enough for Drew to finish his run.

He glanced around the kitchen. "Is she still here?"

I shook my head, noting the way his shoulders dropped as relief settled in. This ghost thing was turning out to be a problem.

"Are we going to be okay?" I had to ask. "I don't plan for this type of thing to happen, but it does." More often than I'd like.

As ghosts went, Summer ranked low on the annoying scale—only showing up around mealtime to offer comments and criticisms on my cooking skills. She hadn't been forthcoming with details about her death—totally normal in my experience—other than to insist she hadn't poisoned anyone.

"Little spooky." At least Drew was honest. "But I think I'll adjust. It would be easier if I could see her for myself. Then I'd know when she's around."

According to Kat Canton—my go-to source for psychic information—ghosts carry the ability but sometimes lack the energy to show themselves to people who normally wouldn't perceive them.

"If you're sure about that, I can talk to Summer and see if she's willing to show herself to you." Or at least try. Kat hadn't taught me how to sense a ghost's level of energy, but I'd seen firsthand that if you made one mad enough, they could move inanimate objects. "But you know how the saying goes, there are things that once seen, cannot be unseen. You need to be sure."

"Sure of what?" Summer shimmered into view. "Oh, sorry. I forgot." She eyed Drew and mimed zipping her lips shut.

Drew didn't answer right away, so I figured I'd give him time to think about what he wanted. In the meantime, I thought Summer deserved to hear Ernie's news.

"Speaking of Summer, she's here now, and there's been a new development. I have sad news. One of her catering customers passed away. Same cause of death."

"Who?" Summer and Drew spoke at the same time.

"Frank Bodine."

The otherworldly sensation of Summer's distress tingled across the back of my neck. The prickling only lasted a second before she redirected her energy toward the stove, turning all the burners on with a whoosh.

Drew flinched. I flinched. Summer wailed. Drew flinched again, and I saw goosebumps spread across his arms. "What was that?"

"Summer's upset." Understandably so.

"That's no excuse." Drew went into practical mode, which told me he wasn't entirely freaked out by Summer's display. "She could have burned the house down if one of us wasn't here to keep an eye on things. Does this happen a lot? I thought you said there was nothing to worry about."

The burners went back out.

"I'm sorry," Regret turned Summer's tone shrill. "I didn't know I could do that. I'll leave, and I won't come back. I didn't mean to cause trouble." Before I could stop her, she was gone.

"It's not safe," Drew had been talking, but I'd tuned him out.

"It's okay, she's gone."

"Like for good?"

"So she says."

Chapter Six

Peanut wants his auntie—Jacy's text came in just after Drew left to teach his evening class. *Meet me at the park?*

Ten minutes—I sent back.

"Hey, Molls! Want to go for a walk?"

In my house, *walk* is a magic word that pushes my dog's wiggle button. Almost seventy pounds of chocolate lab shimmied into the room with her leash in her mouth.

"I'll take that as a yes."

On my way past, I grabbed my roller bottle of Momma Wade's mosquito repellent out of my hiking bag because the bloodsuckers would be out looking for snacks this time of day. I didn't want to come home covered in itchy welts, and her blend of essential oils worked—and smelled—better than anything sold in stores.

Even though we'd walked at a fair clip, Jacy beat us to the park and was pushing Wade's stroller down the paved path toward the picnic tables when Molly caught sight of her. Not wanting to be dragged off my feet, I let go of the leash and watched the big dog lope toward one of her favorite people.

"Hello, Molly." Faintly, Jacy's voice traveled across air laden with humidity. Even more faintly came the silver sound of Wade giggling as Molly's tail thwacked into the side of the stroller. Closer now, I saw his chubby fingers reaching for the tempting item that kept going just beyond his reach. With each swish, he altered his timing until he finally snagged a handful of fur.

Feeling the tug on her anatomy, Molly turned, saw the baby, and rewarded him with a sloppy kiss that only made Wade giggle harder and bounce in his seat.

"Molly's really good with him," Jacy observed as I caught up, and we settled side by side on the seat with our backs against the table. She turned the stroller so Wade could see the show, produced a tennis ball from the storage area under the seat, and gave it a toss sending Molly into frantic motion that delighted the child.

"You said peanut wanted his auntie, but what you really meant was peanut wanted auntie's dog."

"What can I say? You and Molly are a package deal."

"I suppose we are." The dog had come to me a little over a year before when her owner had become the second ghost whose murder I'd had to solve. "We're family now. Speaking of, where's Brian tonight?"

"Tractor-trailer hit that sharp curve on the Hanover road at a bit over the limit. Took down two poles and a section of guardrail before he got control again."

"Anyone hurt?"

"Driver was a bit shook up, but that's it. Brian's out with the crew getting the lines repaired so the folks on the other end can have their air conditioning turned back on. I expect he'll be out half the night."

"Didn't the town put up more signs out there?" I'd heard Martha talking about it in the spring.

Jacy nodded. "Sure did. Four warning signs in each direction aren't enough to stop the idiots from driving too fast. Maybe they thought five would be the charm. Doesn't seem to have worked out that way."

Wade's giggles abruptly turned to annoyed noises. "I'll get him," I said and went to work unstrapping the baby from the stroller. When I lifted him out and held him up to say hello, he made growly noises, grabbed for my ears, and planted his mouth over my nose.

"Ow," I said as his forehead bumped mine. "I think he's hungry."

"No." Jacy laughed. "He's giving kisses."

Going with it, I made smooching sounds that earned more baby giggles. After my marriage ended, I'd decided family life wasn't in the cards for me. Cuddling Wade, I could admit the decision had been ill-timed and hasty.

"I want one of these." I didn't even realize I'd spoken out loud until I saw Jacy's expression change.

"With Drew?" she asked.

"I don't know. We haven't talked about kids. I mean, we've been talking about moving in together for a while now, but things keep getting in the way."

"What do you mean by things?"

"First, I held back because of my ghost problem, but then I ended up telling him about Delly. He seemed fine at the time, but that was weeks ago, and we're still talking about the move in vague terms."

"It's a big step, Ev. And you haven't been together that long, so you need to be sure."

We'd had the conversation before, and I knew she was only looking out for me, but it made me wonder. "Don't you like Drew? If I remember, you're the one who practically pushed me at him."

"Of course, I like him. I've known him since he wore nappies, and he's good people—the best. So are you, and I think you're great together, but it doesn't matter what I think. You need to feel the thing, or it doesn't count. So, the question is, do you feel the thing?"

"If you love me at all, you will stop saying feel the thing. I'm trying to give this moment the gravity it deserves."

Eyebrows waggling, Jacy grinned. "Then I take it you have felt the thing."

My face flamed.

"The thing has been felt," I said, smiling. "But I'm not sure it's down to what I want anymore. I think he's changed his mind now that he's had a ringside seat to me carrying on a conversation with thin air. How does someone get used to that?"

Jacy waved her hand in a dismissive gesture. "Pfft. I talk to myself all the time. Brian finds it charming. If you love someone, you accept their eccentricities. If you can't, then it's not love."

I didn't think it was that simple, but I wished it were. Jacy and Brian were one of those couples that would stand. No matter what life threw at them, they would hold each other up and forge on. My parents were the same way. Once upon a time, I'd thought Paul and I would be the same, but then the blinders came off.

"This thing with Drew is new, and it happened fast," I said. "Maybe too fast."

"Or," Jacy took the counterpoint. "It was just the right time, and you needed the heartbreak with Paul to teach you what you wanted in a mate."

"A mate? As in soul mate? You know I don't believe in that kind of thing." Not anymore.

Looking sad now, Jacy threw the ball for Molly twice before she answered.

"I watch these movies where, when the couple gets together in the end, one of them makes some grand speech about how the other one makes them happier than they ever thought they could be, and do you know what I think when I hear that?"

I shook my head.

"I think what a self-centered idiot, and in real life, the relationship wouldn't last a year." She set the ball down, reached into the bag hanging off the stroller for a baby wipe, and cleaned dog slobber from her fingers. "Impassioned speeches about happiness are fine and romantic, but the true test isn't in the grand gestures. It's in the little things that happen day-to-day. You can't make someone happy; they have to do that for themselves, but you can love them while they figure it out and be there when they need you. That's the secret."

She took the now-sleeping baby from me and settled him back in the stroller. "If he can't handle your ghosts, he's not the right guy for you. If you can't find a way to help him deal, then you're not the right woman for him. Just try not to hurt each other too much while you figure it out."

Sometimes Jacy forgets to put on the velvet glove when she pulls out her iron fist.

Her next comment threw me totally off guard. "Hey! Isn't that Mrs. Tipton sneaking through the bushes over there?"

I looked. "It is."

Given her tendency to dream up town events impossible to pull off without my help, you'd think I'd have had the sense to leave Martha alone if she didn't want to be seen. I did not.

"Molly, stay! I'll be right back."

Of course, Molly didn't stay, and since she's hard to miss when she gets excited, Martha saw me coming.

"Everly, what are you doing here?" If you took Martha at face value, you'd expect a nice, grandmotherly lady who carried mints or butterscotch in her purse and always had tissues. You'd be wrong. Martha was the backbone of Mooselick River and a shameless manipulator of people in her pursuit to make the town great again.

"I'm here with Jacy. We're just visiting. What are you doing here?"

"Oh, I've been trying to get more exercise these days, so I thought I'd go for a walk in the park."

I wasn't buying it.

"You have a twig in your hair," I observed in a dry tone as I picked it out and showed it to her.

Martha puffed up like a chicken in a rainstorm.

"If you must know, I was assessing the damage to the war memorial. It's in a frightful state and needs repair. I'm planning to get an estimate, so I'll know how much money we need to raise to get it fixed."

Translation—Get ready; I'm gearing up to plan another town event.

"The war memorial is on the other end of the park." I could see it from where we stood if I turned my head, and again, I wasn't buying her explanation, so I crossed my arms over my chest and gave her a stern look.

"For Heaven's sake. I was at the memorial when I saw Carolyn Lombardi coming out of the House of Pizza, and I didn't want to argue with her again, so I—" Martha waved a hand toward the bushes she'd dodged through to get into the park.

"Carolyn Lombardi is Thea's mother, right?"

Martha nodded. "The woman is positively deluded. Worse than Bess Tate, and that's saying something."

"About what?" I prodded. She had me curious.

"Land's sake, child, if anyone ought to know, it's you."

My heart lurched. What had I done now? Or worse, what did Martha want me to do?

"Let's pretend I don't."

Martha squinted up at me. "Or maybe you're one of them."

The twists and turns in Martha's logic centers defied geometry. "One of who?"

"Whom," she corrected.

Considering she always said nucular instead of nuclear, she probably shouldn't be correcting my grammar. I held back a derisive grunt. "All right, then. Whom."

"Do you think Summer Merryfield murdered Frank Bodine in cold blood?" Martha cocked her head to the side and waited for me to respond.

"I don't."

"Well, good. At least you're not an idiot. But there's plenty who are. People I'd have sworn were decent, God-fearing folk have set out to prove me wrong. Can you believe anyone would want to deny that poor girl a church funeral?"

On the best of days, Martha's brain went around like a pea in a whistle, so it took me a second to follow her thought process and come to the most logical conclusion.

"Summer?" My face went hot with indignation as I caught up. "Because they think she's a murderer?"

"Doesn't that beat all?" Martha squeaked. "I'm livid. I might have to leave the church if they go through with this ridiculous travesty. I don't know what is wrong with people. Summer Merryfield almost single-handedly supplied the last three bake sales and wouldn't take a penny for the ingredients. And this is how they repay her generosity? By branding her a killer and deciding she's not good enough to go through the church doors feet-first?"

That sounded unfair to me since there wasn't a shred of evidence that Summer had done anything wrong, and I said so.

"This will mean dire things for the whole town, you mark my words," she said. "Dire things."

On that note, I left Martha to make her way back to the pizza place to see if Carolyn had gone.

"What was that all about? It looked like Martha was in a tizzy," Jacy idly pushed the stroller back and forth with one hand to keep the baby sleeping while she sat with her feet in front of her, ankles crossed.

"Martha idles at tizzy." I flapped a hand. "I guess Carolyn Lombardi has decided to brand Summer a murderer and is doing her best to talk the church people into denying Summer a proper funeral. Isn't that archaic?"

I was shocked that Jacy wasn't surprised.

"Well, there's not a lot Carolyn wouldn't stoop to since she's nastier than pond scum, but she's not the only one on that particular crazy train."

"What do you mean?" I shifted to face Jacy while she explained.

"We get a lot of locals in the shop, and Summer's a hot topic." She paused to frame her words kindly. "People are saying just awful things about her."

"What kinds of things?" I flinched when Summer's voice sounded loud right behind my left ear. I spun my head to see her sitting cross-legged on the picnic table, her face a mask of displeasure. I guessed her embargo of me only pertained to my house. Fine by me.

My stern look registered with her about as well as my talk on the rules—basically, not at all.

"She's here, isn't she?" Jacy looked at the point where I'd focused, saw the empty table, then back at me. Her hand left the stroller and fluttered to her mouth. "No, don't tell me."

"Okay, I won't."

"But tell me. She's here, right?" Her breath whistled when Jacy sucked it in. "A real, live, honest-to-goodness ghost is sitting right next to me."

"Any chance she'll calm down soon?" Summer cocked a brow, crossed her arms, and waited.

I shrugged. "Give her a minute."

"What? Who? Me?" If she kept on swiveling her head that quickly, Jacy would need a massage and maybe a chiropractor.

"Enough." I put my hands up, palms out toward each of them. "Jacy, Summer wants to know what people have been saying about her."

"Oh."

I saw the wheels turning in Jacy's head. We'd been friends since basically forever, and I knew what she was thinking. It was one thing to tell me the hurtful gossip, and quite another to say those same things in front of Summer.

"Well," she paused to find a way to frame it gently, and then Jacy focused on a spot just over Summer's left shoulder. "I guess...it was just...okay, before I say anything else, you should know that I don't believe you poisoned Frank because he caught you in bed with Margo and threatened to divorce her because she engaged in the forbidden act of love with another woman."

I choked. "In the what?"

"Don't make me say it again."

Summer closed her eyes and shook her head for a moment, then said. "I guess I know who started that one. My next-door neighbor has a twisted mind. Is that the worst of it?"

I repeated the question so Jacy could hear it.

"Depends on your outlook, I suppose. If you weren't sleeping with Margo, I figure you also weren't sleeping with Frank, and neither was your husband...sleeping with Frank or Margo. I've heard it both ways." Now that she'd warmed up, Jacy couldn't seem to stop. "There's more in the same line, but I think I'd better move on to stuff that doesn't involve having to ask if you had a sex swing installed in your basement because that isn't the worst of it."

Summer's rising anger prickled across my skin. I shivered.

"Just nutshell it for us, Jacy. Please."

"Okay." She took a deep breath and plunged in. "There's a theory floating around that Summer has been killing off people for years using poisons that couldn't be detected, and she only got caught this time because she got cocky and didn't give Margo enough to kill her. And she ended up dead because of some sort of divine retribution. Or else she got careless."

For one unbearable moment, Summer's energy ramped up to the point where it caused me actual pain, then she got herself under control.

"Thank Jacy for me," was all she said before she faded.

"But you have to know, I don't believe any of that crap. No one who has half a brain believes it. And for every wild story, there were just as many people who said really lovely things."

"She's gone, Jace. But I'll tell her later."

"Good. I didn't want to hurt her feelings, and for a minute there, I was pretty sure I felt something spooky." Holding up her arm, Jacy pointed to the tiny bumps still standing there. "Freaky deaky."

"Congratulations, you just had your first ghostly encounter."

"It's probably a good thing we didn't mention that business with the funeral."

I agreed.

Chapter Seven

"This is becoming a regular thing," I dropped my paintbrush in the jar of water I'd been using to clean it between colors. Watching David bring his "painted lady" of an inn back to life had inspired me to finish a few projects around my own place. Since I'm not particularly crafty, I figured I'd start by adding some bright color to my porch posts' turned details.

"Does this look familiar to you?" Ernie flipped his hand over and uncurled his fingers. My stomach dropped because the answer was yes. I recognized the bottle in his palm for two reasons. For one thing, I'd seen it sitting on the counter in Summer's kitchen. Secondly, from this close, I could read the label.

"That's one of Leandra's concoctions," I said in dismay, though I supposed I shouldn't have been surprised since Jacy had mentioned her mother and Summer had known each other. "Angelica extract. Did you have it tested?"

Leandra, or Momma Wade—she'd made me call her that when I was younger, and sometimes, I still did—was the type of person who carried spiders outside rather than killing them. If she'd made a mistake and brewed up something that had killed two people and possibly a third, I wasn't sure she could live with her conscience.

"I sent a sample to an independent lab." He held the bottle up to the light and frowned. "On my own dime, I might add. Had to do it by mail, so it's looking like it will take a week. Maybe two."

Plenty of time for the killer to cover his tracks. Or hers. "Is it true that poison is usually a woman's weapon? It seems like such a cliché. Or would that be an adage?"

Ernie shrugged. "Adages generally have their roots in the truth, but in this case, I'd call it more of a mistaken assumption. It all comes down to intent, doesn't it?"

Gesturing for him to follow me, I went inside to wash my hands.

"There's a theory," he continued, "that Lucrezia Borgia was merely a pawn rather than the predator she's been painted throughout history. It's likely the men in her family decided who would die and coerced her into using their chosen weapon."

Look at him studying crime throughout the ages.

"Poison in the right hand is only used to kill weeds. I wouldn't discount anyone based on gender."

"I see your point," I said.

"But if this," he said, holding the bottle up again, "was the source, Vinnie could be right, and we're looking at an accident."

I reached for the bottle, Ernie held it back, so I wiggled my fingers impatiently until he reluctantly complied. There was something I knew about Leandra's methods that maybe he didn't.

"You see this notation at the bottom of the label?" I pointed to where it was marked 7/30 in fine pen next to a stamp of a sun in purple ink.

"Sure, I figured that was the date."

"It's not." I pointed to the sun stamp. "That's the date. She uses a different stamp for each month and a different colored ink each year. She says she can keep track at a glance that way. This is bottle seven of a batch of thirty."

"Thirty? There are thirty bottles of possible poison out there?"

That was all he needed to hear. Ernie headed for the door with me on his heels. "I'm going with you." And I wasn't taking no for an answer.

He didn't argue.

"Are you going to run the siren?" I asked as I buckled up.

"Are you a child?" He backed out of the driveway and did not turn on the siren. Bummer.

We found Leandra ankle-deep in a pile of partially composted manure she was turning over with a pitchfork. When she saw me coming, her face lit up, then when she saw Ernie, her expression turned fearful.

"What happened? Is it Jacy?"

"No, she's fine. Everyone's fine." Well, except for Summer and Frank, and possibly Margo. "We just need to talk to you about something."

"Maybe we could go," Ernie looked for a spot well away from the manure. "Over there." He gestured vaguely toward a garden bench closer to the house and downwind of the smell.

"Okay." Now that she knew none of her family was in danger, Leandra smiled cheerfully beneath her straw hat. Once clear of the manure pile, she stepped out of the rainbow-patterned rubber boots she'd worn for the job and padded across the grass with bare feet. "You sit right down, I'll bring us some lemonade, and then we'll talk about whatever it is that brought you out here on this fine day."

I suspected she needed a minute to settle herself, but I wouldn't say no to a cold drink, and her lemonade rated high among my all-time favorite beverages. She always added a bit of muddled mint that made the drink even more refreshing.

"No, it's—" Ernie was too late to stop the mini-tornado headed for her kitchen.

When she returned, I took a sip while Ernie pulled out the little glass bottle of extract and set it on the table. He spun it so Leandra could see the label. "This is yours, right?" He pushed his lemonade toward the middle of the table as if trying to get it out of arm's reach.

Squinting for a moment, Leandra fished around the front pocket of her bibbed denim overalls and pulled a pair of drug-store cheaters to help get a closer look.

"I made this if that's what you're asking." She pulled off the glasses and looked up at Ernie. "Why?"

"You sold this to Summer Merryfield," Ernie stated rather than questioned, and it came out sounding like an accusation more than anything else.

"Sold? No," Leandra sipped her lemonade, her expression turning colder than the ice in her glass. "We split the batch since we made it together. Why?"

The last thing I wanted was Leandra mad at me. I didn't call her Momma Wade just because she asked me to, but because I'd spent a large portion of my childhood running tame in her home. She was my second mother. I only meant to nudge Ernie's leg with my toe but managed to kick him a little harder than I planned.

"How would you go about making an extract like this? Is it a complicated process?"

"Easy as anything, but it takes some time." Ernie got a sidelong glance, and I figured Leandra had a pretty good idea why we'd come asking questions, but she answered mine without hesitation. "To make an extract, simply chop the leaves of whatever plant you're using, put them in a jar, and cover with grain alcohol. Let the mixture steep for a week or two, strain off the liquid, and add more leaves. Rinse and repeat once or even twice more depending on how strong you want your extract."

I got a final smile, which dropped off her face as she turned back to Ernie and said, "And before you ask, neither one of us was dumb enough to put hemlock in with the angelica. We did add some edible flower petals to enhance the floral notes, and maybe another secret ingredient or two. I suppose you'll want a full list for your report."

Ernie held up both hands in surrender. "Calm down, Mrs. Wade."

You'd think the man would learn by now that telling a woman to calm down generally had about the same effect as tossing a match into dry tinder. To be fair, Leandra didn't shout or gesticulate wildly. She kept her fury contained, but you could see it in her short, jerky motions and in the fire in her eyes.

One eyebrow quirked, Leandra's gaze never left Ernie's face as she deliberately reached for the glass bottle still sitting in the middle of the table. Before either of us realized what she intended to do, she'd twisted off the cap, held the bottle aloft in a sort of salute, then tipped the contents into her mouth. A gulp and a swallow, and if there was poison in the mix, I'd just killed Jacy's mother.

Talk about blood running cold. Mine turned to icy streams that I could feel slipping through every vein.

"Thus, with a kiss," she blew a smooching sound as she quoted Shakespeare in Ernie's direction, "I die."

"Leandra Wade," his voice roared. "You damn fool. What were you thinking?"

Now, who needed to be told to calm down? I resisted the temptation and hoped she knew what she was doing.

"Relax." Leandra leaned back on her chair. "I'm not going to die." Then she leaned forward again and shoved the bottle under Ernie's nose. "What do you smell?"

He pulled back out of reflex, then breathed in. "Alcohol and flowers."

Nodding, Leandra said, "Exactly. Angelica smells like flowers. Do you know what brewed hemlock smells like?"

"I can't say as I do."

"Musty mouse piss."

My lemonade went down hard as the look on Ernie's face nearly made me choke.

"Summer would have known the difference?" Now that the crisis moment was over, Ernie delved for more information. That's what makes him a better cop than most people give him credit for. He's always thinking.

With an exaggerated eye-roll, Leandra nodded. "Of course, she knew. If you're thinking she accidentally poisoned anyone, you might want to consider another line of work. Maybe take up a job that doesn't require you to think or puts people's lives in your hands."

Feet splayed out under the table, Ernie settled back in his chair but let the insult pass. Another point in his favor—being slow to take offense.

"If it makes you feel any better, I don't think Summer killed anyone—on purpose or otherwise."

It surprised me that he was willing to put his opinion out there so boldly. As much as I loved Jacy's mother, I wouldn't tell her anything I didn't want half the town to know. Or maybe that was his intention. Let it leak how he didn't think Summer was behind the deaths and see what types of dust bunnies came creeping out from under the furniture.

"And yet, here you are with your puffed-up self." Leandra took off her hat, used it to fan her face. "Throwing accusations around."

"I had to follow up." Ernie glanced at me, scowled when he saw my incredulous look. He did, too, think, at least for a minute or two, there were thirty bottles of poison floating around. I didn't tell Leandra that, though.

"I'm glad to hear you say that," she said. "Because at the time when we brewed this batch of extract, Summer was in her careful phase."

I frowned. "What do you mean by careful?"

"You know, the kind of person who thinks twice, speaks once," Leandra said as if that explained everything.

It didn't. Not exactly.

"You mean thoughtful," I said. To my mind, there was a distinction.

"No, I mean careful. Watchful. Maybe guarded is a better word, you know? Her energy signature—" Leandra broke off to glare at Ernie when he made a derisive sound. "Was a little low. But then, we all vibrate at a different frequency, don't we? Some people," she gave the still-smirking policeman a pointed look, "Are quiet because they're like sponges absorbing the energy of those around them. Taking it all in and holding it there until they can let it out a little at a time and just when needed."

Ernie could think what he liked about Leandra's spirit guides and her talk of energies and chakras and whatever else she came up with. I had good reason to know there was some power in her oils and whatnot.

Still, in my dealings with her, I hadn't found Summer to be shy, so Leandra's description didn't make sense, but I let her continue.

"Some are more like mirrors. They don't emit much in their own right but reflect the life force of others."

Since Leandra seemed to be gearing up for a longer lecture, I tried to derail by asking, "Which category would you say Summer fit into?"

A moment passed before the answer came. "Neither, I guess. Summer was more like an egg. Delicate and breakable. Fragile, almost. Careful of what she said and what she did. Careful not to let her light show through her shell. The funny thing about shells is they might be protective, but they also wall a person off from everything life has to offer."

Using fanciful language, Leandra had described someone who hunched in on herself and walled out the world. Someone who lived in fear. Not the Summer I knew.

"You knew her better, I suppose, but I find her to be bubbly and outgoing," I said.

My slip earned me a barefooted kick under the table. There was a lot of that going around.

"Found, I mean. She seemed talkative the day I met her." I glanced at Ernie to see if he noticed anything, but it didn't seem like it. I could probably tell him flat-out that I sometimes see ghosts, and he wouldn't believe me anyway.

Momma Wade knew my secret since her spiritual meddling with something she called my third eye was the reason I could see them in the first place. She'd been trying to help me, but she'd done more damage than good, and my life would never be the same.

"Could be she was only nervous around you," I said, hoping Leandra wouldn't take offense. "Running a catering business and a café takes a certain amount of comfortability around people."

"Well, sure." I was surprised when Leandra agreed with me. "As I said, that was at the time we made the extract. She opened up a lot after she struck out on her own. To stick with the egg metaphor, she came out of her shell. Her energy emerged full-blown from the cocoon of her psyche."

The pronouncement came in an exuberant tone and with a series of dramatic hand gestures that made Ernie's mouth twitch at the corners. He covered his face with his hand for a moment to get control of his expression. If not for my years of practice around Momma Wade's theatrics, I might have needed to follow suit.

But Leandra had me thinking. The way she described Summer set off warning bells in my head. You don't do fundraising for a charitable foundation without getting an education on recognizing a battered woman. I couldn't be sure without asking, but Leandra's description fit the bill perfectly.

Jack Merryfield's distress at his former wife's death had seemed genuine at the time, but he could have been putting on a front. It happens. Drawing his face out of memory, I played the experience back and forth to see if there had been any clues and only came back to the present when a new thought hit me.

"What about Summer's family? Did she talk about her folks at all?"

A bird chirped in the silence that followed while Leandra gave the matter some thought.

"Barely. I think her father either died or left when Summer was young because she only ever mentioned her mother. I got the impression there was a rift between them, but that's it."

"We should probably," Ernie said, "let Mrs. Wade get back to her gardening." What he meant was he'd hit his limit of woo-woo for the day.

I rose to follow him out, but then he stopped and turned back.

"Do you think you could show me where you and Summer harvested the angelica?"

Leandra froze. Only for a second, but the slight narrowing of Ernie's eyes said he'd caught the moment of hesitation, too.

"I'm sorry, I can't. I wasn't with her at the time, and I have no idea where she found it."

Once in the car, he sighed, but we barely spoke all the way back to my place. I'd decided not to share my suspicions about Jack until I confirmed with Summer. No sense in pointing the finger until I had something concrete to go on.

"Leandra lied," was all he said when he pulled to a stop in my driveway.

"I know," was all I answered, but I figured he wanted me to find out why.

Chapter Eight

"No. Don't do that," I told Drew when he called to offer to cancel his evening classes so he could sit with me the night before Paul's trial. "I'll order in something spicy from Bertie's, throw on my rattiest clothes, and watch movies you hate to take my mind off of things."

Not having him around would actually be less stressful, I thought, but I didn't want to hurt his feelings. Drew tuned in more than most men, probably because his self-defense practice showed him the benefits of paying close attention to his surroundings. He wouldn't mean to add to my burden of worry, but even solicitous regard carried extra weight.

A few hours of solitude and chick flicks should level me out, and if I wanted to dance along to the soundtracks of eighties movies, there'd be no one there to look at me funny.

Not even Summer, who hadn't shown her face in the house since she'd said she wouldn't. Fine by me. The discussion of her ex could wait until after I'd had to deal with mine. Hers wasn't in a position to do more damage. Mine was.

If I let him, which I didn't plan to do.

With my evening plans resolved, I ordered both pasta and a personal sized-pizza—a girl has to have options—and half the dessert menu from Bertino's, then took Molly out for a rousing game of fetch while I waited for the food to arrive.

I tired of the game and the slobber-coated tennis ball long before Molly had had enough, so between throws, wandered over to the end of the back porch to nip off the end of a stalk of what Summer insisted was oregano. The patch had grown nearly half again in size during the time I'd lived here. Former owner, Catherine, had probably taken pains to keep it in check.

In fact, as I glanced around the backyard, I figured she might frown on my haphazard attempts at maintaining her flower beds. I'd never so much as thought about peeking into the backyard of Spooky Manor until I owned the place, but I doubted my efforts compared to hers. While Catherine had been a bit of a hidden hoarder, she'd kept her home's outward face organized enough most people had no clue about the clutter behind the scenes. It was a safe bet her backyard hadn't looked like it did now.

"The extension office offers classes in gardening," My mother's voice made me jump and drop the leaves I'd been sniffing, coming as it did, unexpectedly from just inside the open door off the kitchen. I hadn't heard her pull in or let herself into the house.

"You shouldn't sneak up on people like that," I scolded. "You scared me half to death."

Dressed in a pair of Capri pants and a sleeveless blouse, my mother looked she'd stepped out of an ad for antiperspirant. Whatever gene it was that kept her looking crisp and clean even at the end of her workday was not one she'd passed down to me. Next to her, I always felt like I'd been left in the dryer too long and came out wrinkled.

She came over and settled on the top step—a thing I'd never dare in light clothes, but dirt rarely seemed to stick to Kitty Dupree. I went and sat beside her.

"Sorry," she said. "I just wanted to check in and see if you'd changed your mind. I'm happy to go with you tomorrow for moral support."

A little over a year before, she probably wouldn't have offered, and I certainly wouldn't have considered—as I was now—saying yes. Our relationship had changed since I moved back to town, and I liked that we'd become closer.

"You just want to be there if by some miracle Paul is convicted so you can see him hauled off to jail." I nudged her shoulder with mine. Part of our former schism had come from her not hiding her opinion of my former husband while we were married. She'd been right about him, too, but hadn't thrown her rightness in my face after the split, which had gone a long way toward healing the one between her and me.

"Merely a side benefit, my love." She put her hand on my knee and squeezed gently. "I promise to only gloat a little. Internally. You know, like that thing with ducks where all the paddling goes on under the surface."

I snorted at the mental image. "I appreciate the offer, but I'll be fine. You don't have to take a day off just to play the gloating duck for me." She'd just gone back to work after using up several years' worth of saved up personal days. I didn't want her taking more time off for something I could handle on my own.

"Your father—" she began.

"It's okay, Mom. I won't be alone, Patrea will be with me, and I'll be less nervous just knowing you're both there in spirit."

Less embarrassed, too, if neither of my parents had to hear the story of how I'd found Paul the day Reva tried to kill me. Seeing my father's reaction to it might kill the amusement value of that memory for me.

"As much as I appreciate your support, this is just something I need to do by myself. Do you understand?"

"Of course." She gave in without argument. Another sign our relationship had changed for the better. "But I feel like I need to do something." She sat in silent contemplation while I rose from my seat on the steps and tossed Molly's ball a few more times.

When I turned back, it was to see my mother staring at me intently.

"I wasn't planning to go to court looking like this." I'd seen that look before.

"I should hope not, but you need to do something with your hair. It looks…" she struggled to find a kind word. "A little unkempt."

My hand went up to tangle in the curly mess that I'd let grow out long over the past few months.

"I'm trying something new." It came out sounding more defensive than I'd thought it would.

For the first six months after the split, I'd driven back to the city every few weeks to get my hair trimmed and shaped the way Paul had liked it best. A habit it hadn't occurred to me to bother breaking until I realized I could. When I decided to rebel, I'd stopped going to the salon entirely, which I admit was a quick zoom right past the middle ground.

Now, my hair hung a good three inches longer than it had before, and I mostly wore it pulled back in a tail or braid to keep it out of my face. Unkempt was as good a description as any.

"I'll call Peggy and see if she can squeeze you in first thing in the morning."

Peggy. The same Peggy who was supposed to marry Summer's ex-husband?

"Okay. Why not?"

Mom beamed at being able to do something, even something small, to help me, and went inside to make the call. I gave Molly one last toss and arrived back in my kitchen just in time to hear her thank Peggy and hang up.

"It's all set. The salon opens at nine, and I know you have to be at the courthouse by ten, so I called in a favor and got Peggy to go in early. You need to be there at eight. That should leave plenty of time for a wash, cut, and dry, at least."

"Thanks, Mom." It should also give me time to ask a few subtle questions about Jack. If he'd mistreated Summer, he might be doing the same with Peggy. A sobering thought, and one I needed to put off until later.

Satisfied she'd done all she could, my mother gave me a firm hug, a kiss on the forehead, and met the Bertino's delivery on her way out.

"What on earth did you order?" She said when she saw the number of bags. "One of everything?"

"Not quite, but close." I paid the bill, added a generous tip, and nearly swooned at the scent of spicy sauce. "There's plenty if you want to stay."

She declined, then followed the delivery guy back down the front steps, muttering something about people who could eat like that and not lose their figure as she went. When both vehicles had gone, I carried the food inside and settled down to watch Flashdance in peace.

Chapter Nine

"I just love this color," Peggy Sullivan practically gushed as she ran her hands through my tangle of curls. "Medium copper blond with an overlay of crimson flame to get that Balayage effect, right?" She winked at me in the mirror as if we shared some secret.

"What?"

"That's your blend of shades, right? Or should I say *our* blend of shades? I have an eye for these things. An eye for dye, I guess you could say, and I'm never wrong." Peggy selected a steel comb that looked like she'd stolen it off a dog groomer and felt like a torture device as she dragged it through my hair. "They did a first-rate job. I can't hardly see any new growth near the roots."

"It's my natural color." I winced when she hit a tangle and yanked hard.

"Sure, honey. I won't tell if you won't. Now, what can I do for you?"

I hadn't been in her chair five minutes, and she'd already managed to strike fear in me. I mean, I wanted to solve Summer's murder, but I wouldn't say it was worth letting Peggy take scissors to my hair.

"You know how to do a blowout, right? I'm fine with the length. I just want it to look sleek and polished."

"You could stand to lose an inch or two. Maybe three. And it could do with some shaping, but you're the boss." Peggy got me all trussed up in a black plastic cape and guided me over to the shampoo sink. The water was a little warmer than I liked. Otherwise, she did a pretty good job of things. Good enough to lull me into thinking this might turn out okay so long as I could get her talking on the topic of Summer's ex.

"I have to go to court today, and I confess I'm a little nervous because my ex-husband will be there."

The steel comb felt marginally better now that the liberal amount of conditioner she'd used smoothed its path.

"Men." Peggy rolled her eyes. "Am I right?" She tugged harder on the comb.

Seemed like Peggy didn't recognize me from gushing over her wedding plans at Cappy's. Also sounded like there might be trouble in paradise. I gave a little nod, which she took as encouragement.

"My fiancé decided to move back into the house he shared with his ex-wife. He didn't even bother to ask me what I thought of the idea. He's over there packing up her things right now, and I'm supposed to give notice today whether I want to or not. I hate to have to tell my landlord.

She's so nice, but I just know I'll lose my security deposit. And does he care?"

She answered her own question. "No, he does not. If he did, he'd have told me his name was still on the mortgage at her place, too. These are things a wife should know about her husband. Or her husband-to-be, even."

Tug. Tug. Ouch.

Peggy was on a roll with the comb and with her rant. I'd wanted information, but I hadn't expected to have to pay for it in pain.

"They had an amicable divorce." Peggy's air quotes came off awkward and, frankly, a bit scary because she had the comb in one hand and had picked up her scissors with the other. I wasn't sure whether to commiserate with her or duck in case she got too close and lopped of an earlobe or something. "What does that even mean? Do you know?"

I could honestly admit I did not.

Peggy said, "I'll tell you what he says it means. He says they're friends. Or they were. She's dead, and she still has her hooks in him. Can you imagine what it would be like to have to move into a house full of things someone else picked out?"

As a matter of fact, I could. I could also see her point about not wanting to live with the memory of his ex jumping out at her from every corner. You can probably see the irony in the situation, given I had his actual ex jumping out at me from every corner.

"You are an idiot." This from the hairdresser at the next station as she arranged things the way she wanted them in preparation for her first client of the day. "Everyone knows Jack Merryfield killed his wife so he wouldn't have to keep paying alimony. You should dump his ass before he does the same to you."

"I am not an idiot, and a fat lot you know about things. He wasn't even paying her alimony," Peggy's voice took on a so-there tone. "She wouldn't take money from him. Said she was doing things her way, and her pride was worth more than money."

Internally, I applauded Summer for her take on things.

Cindy—I caught a look at her name tag—curled her lip, rolled her eyes. "It's always the husband."

With short, angry motions that made me cringe, Peggy picked up a blow dryer and fitted a many-fingered attachment to it. She flicked the switch and came at me with the heat-belching appliance. I cringed again.

I've had plenty of blowouts before, but this one wasn't like any of the others as Peggy pressed the finger attachment against my head and made circular motions that reminded me of twirling spaghetti on a fork.

The next five minutes had me forgetting my reason for coming here and that Summer ever existed. As Peggy dried and swirled, swirled and dried, my hair got wilder and curlier instead of sleek and straight.

"Um, this isn't…"

"Oh, don't you worry, honey. I'm only getting started here."

Great. Just what I was afraid of.

The dryer ran for twenty minutes before Peggy switched over to a curling iron. When she reached for it, she turned her arm just right, and I saw a blotchy red patch that ended in a straight line just above her wrist.

"That looks sore," I commented when she saw I'd noticed.

"Hazard of the job," Peggy said. "I burn myself on these curling irons all the time. Seems like it just gets healed up a little, and there I go again. But don't worry. Just because I'm a klutz doesn't mean I burn clients or that I can't do good hair."

I'd have begged to differ if I thought it would do me any good. Instead, I watched helplessly as she sectioned my hair and attacked each strand with the curling iron. The appliance's heat smoothed out the curls, turning them into a shining cascade of ringlets rather than a bunch of frizzy ripples.

I had to admit, I looked good when she was done, even if she'd given me the total opposite of the sleek, understated style I'd wanted. I'd planned to go to court looking serious, trustworthy, professional. Somehow, the mane of curls turned my most matronly suit into something else.

"There you go, honey." Peggy tweaked a curl into place. "You look like a million bucks."

I looked like sex on a stick.

Which was, apparently, the look Peggy had been going for. She leaned in and almost whispered in my ear. "And that's how you make a man eat his heart out for being idiot enough to let a good woman go."

Okay, well, I hadn't thought of it quite that way. Peggy earned herself a tip.

Chapter Ten

"What have you done to your hair?" Patrea hissed when she met me on the steps of the courthouse.

"Mooselick River blowout. Don't ask." With no time to go home and attempt damage control, I'd decided to embrace the style.

Patrea did not want to get on board with the plan. "You look like you should be dancing on a pole." Then she squinted at me. "You're not experimenting with styles for the wedding, are you?"

"Thanks. Because that helps my nerves a lot, and no, this is a one-time thing."

We went through the metal detectors and took our place in a bank of uncomfortable, plastic seats outside the courtroom to wait until the Bailiff called Paul's case. He was nowhere to be seen, and for that, I thanked whatever angels watched over me. That feeling lasted right up until a familiar figure turned the corner.

"Drew, what are you doing here?"

He took in my new hairdo, quirked a brow at it. Great, I thought, now he thinks I went out of my way to look good for Paul.

"I thought I'd rack up some supportive boyfriend points," Drew said. He settled on the static-inducing chair next to mine and gave me a quick kiss. "Riley's taking my morning classes, so I'm available until noon. She told me to tell you to kick some serious testimonial butt."

I smiled. "I'll give it my best shot." At least his presence gave me something else to think about while we waited. Did I want him here? Why had he come? Did he think I looked like a pole-dancer, too? Should I ask him? That one had an easy answer. No. Definitely no.

Nothing like trading one set of worries for another.

Drew knew the story of how my marriage ended abruptly the day I'd come home to find my ex in bed with my former friend. He knew how that former friend had tried to frame me for fraud. How she'd killed Winston Durham and tried to frame me for that, too. Then, she'd locked Paul up in a hotel room and come after me. That hadn't worked out so well for her—may she rot in jail forever.

Reva McKinnon was a piece of work.

I'd rather have faced her than my ex across a courtroom any day of the week, and twice on Sunday. Even with him knowing all about my past, having Drew at the trial wouldn't help, I didn't think. The only thing that did was knowing this would be the last time Paul could do anything to screw with my new life.

Once we walked through those doors, I was on my own. I wasn't a material witness or a party to the lawsuit, so my part should be painless. A simple recitation of the facts as I knew them.

Because everything that had to do with Paul turned out to be simple.

Right.

It felt like hours before the door opened, and we were directed to enter the courtroom, but my watch said it hadn't been ten minutes.

Already seated at the defense table, Paul turned when I walked in—his gaze sweeping over me as if he'd never seen me before, his jaw tightening when he saw Drew's hand on the small of my back. How dare he? My temper flared like someone tossed a lit match into a puddle of gasoline—hot and smoky. My chin went up a notch, and I stared him down until he looked away.

Oddly, the heat of the moment burned the edges off my nerves, straightened my spine, and cleared my head. When we took our seats behind the prosecuting attorney, I ended up sitting between Drew and Patrea. On Patrea's other side sat the two FBI agents I'd met when I was the subject of investigation. SSI Martine Coville offered me a brief nod, then turned her attention back toward the proceedings.

"All rise," the Bailiff ordered and introduced the judge. I forgot his name almost as soon as I heard it. Maybe my nerves weren't entirely settled.

The judge invited the prosecuting attorney to make her opening statements. She kept it short and to the point. Whether or not Paul had been the mastermind behind the scheme, she planned to convince the jury he had committed several counts of embezzlement and fraud.

Then Colin Peterson, defense attorney, rose and painted a rather unflattering picture of a man led around by his...um...well, you get the idea.

"They're playing the idiot card," Patrea whispered in my ear.

I'd like to think I'm not bitter, but I totally am because the first thought that popped into my head was that they were playing with a stacked deck in Paul's case. The snort I held back turned into a wince when the defense attorney began to enumerate all the ways Paul and his family had helped the less fortunate, had provided a boon to the community. Then he went on to say Paul had been a victim, even going so far as to mention how his marriage had ended because of Reva and her conniving ways.

"With malice and aforethought, Reva McKinnon set her sights on Paul Hastings. She had only one intention in mind: to perpetrate a con game that would eventually cost him everything, including a happy marriage to the love of his life, his social standing, his place in the family company, and even his freedom."

Sure, that's what happened. Reva twitched her ... little finger—what did you think I was going to say? — and Paul had no choice but to fling off his clothes and climb into bed with her. Takes two to Tango, pal. I bit my tongue and wished I actually did have something to help the prosecutor make her case.

Love of his life. What a load of crap.

"The prosecution will try to convince you that Mr. Hastings was a willing participant in Ms. McKinnon's plans," he faced the jury and made his plea. "But you're all good people. Who among you hasn't trusted the wrong person at least once in your life? When you think about those times when you listened to someone who didn't have your best interests at heart, I know you will see the truth and return a verdict of not guilty."

By the end of Peterson's speech, I'd begun to vibrate in my seat. This was the man Patrea said made a habit out of tearing apart witness testimony. And yet, he'd just called me the love of Paul's life. He wouldn't come at me from the front; Patrea had already made that clear. So, what was his plan?

The wait to find out was interminable. There was donor testimony to wade through, most of which Peterson managed to downplay. Then the prosecutor introduced a forensic accountant named Harold Farraday, who couldn't have been drier if he were made of talcum powder and week-old bread.

Mr. Farraday droned on and on about the most inane aspects of the foundation's bookkeeping until almost every person on jury stared with eyes glazed over from boredom. Even the judge yawned once.

Peterson brought out his own accountant, who made a huge deal out of postulating that the entire case was based on a mistake and suggesting the discrepancies were nothing more than a series of clerical errors. In the most condescending way possible, he called both Farraday's methods and his abilities into question. Farraday made a valiant attempt to stand his ground through sheer, pigheaded repetition.

After what felt like an hour of grandstanding, I pitied the jury for having to try and follow Peterson's verbal contortions. According to him, Paul had been duped into doing something he knew was wrong, except he hadn't actually been duped because the thing that was done wrong was a clerical error. I wanted to stand up and scream for Peterson to pick a defense just go with it. Maybe his whole strategy was to dazzle the jury with so much BS they'd give up and declare Paul not guilty out of desperation.

The sooner, the better, as far as I was concerned. I wanted off the emotional seesaw.

It didn't help my nerves that the judge called a recess for lunch just before it was my turn to testify. By that time, the trial seemed all but over, and, as Patrea had predicted, it looked like Paul would walk.

By unspoken agreement, we didn't discuss the case while we ate, and I kissed Drew goodbye with relief thinking his would be one less set of eyes on me while I testified.

All too soon, it was time to go back into the courtroom, and the prosecuting attorney called me to the stand. Paul's eyes bored into mine, a silent plea for mercy as I put my hand on the Bible and pledged to speak the truth as I knew it.

As rehearsed, the prosecuting attorney took me through the series of events. I even managed to maintain a level tone while describing the duties I had performed during my tenure as director, focusing on the one piece of testimony she considered relevant to her case.

"I organized events that raised funds but had no part in collecting or dispersing those funds. That was basically considered above my pay grade."

"And you didn't find that an odd set of circumstances given your position within the foundation as well as in the family?"

Wasn't that the question I should have been asking myself the entire time I'd worked for the Hastings family?

"In retrospect, I suppose I should have, but I didn't have any frame of reference, so it never occurred to me to raise the question."

She asked me to describe how Paul had come to offer me the job, which I dutifully explained even though it made me feel foolish for not knowing better. But he'd said I was family, and family did their duty. Throwing parties and events was where I fit best in the grand scheme, and I'd been darned good at it, too.

"Isn't it true your husband deliberately kept you sheltered from the financial workings of the foundation?"

The defense objected on the grounds of hearsay, so the prosecutor rephrased, but even I could tell this line of questioning wasn't getting her anywhere. Unless he'd known her for longer than I thought, whatever Paul had or had not done under Reva's influence had begun after she moved into the neighborhood. At least two years after I'd taken on the job at the foundation.

When pressed, I admitted that I didn't think establishing my role in the company had been entirely under Paul's purview, but his father, Thurston, wasn't the one on trial.

I considered myself pretty good at reading people, with the notable exception of my ex-husband and ex-friend. The jury—mainly made up of women—seemed inclined to let Paul slide. He was, I had good reason to know, a fine-looking man who could turn on the charm when he wanted to. A shark like Colin Peterson would have counted on that ability and stacked the jury in his favor.

All he had to do was put Paul on the stand and let him talk.

The prosecutor had one Hail Mary pass to throw and introduced the entire set of documents with my forged signature, including the additions to the prenuptial agreement and the bank account paperwork Paul and Reva had tried to use to set me up as a scapegoat within the foundation.

That got the jury's attention, and the dance began.

I was asked to step down but cautioned to remember that I was still under oath. The defense declared the forgeries fake—how was that for irony? The prosecution called an expert to the stand; the defense called another.

Peterson's expert was good, but the FBI's was better. I sat stoically under the scrutiny of the jury, knowing most of those women probably thought I was a fool.

When it came to Paul, I agreed with them.

Paul sat diagonally to my right, his spine stiff, his jaw set. I couldn't see his parents without turning my head, but I felt them there and knew exactly what I'd see on their faces if I did turn: haughty disdain. As if they were the ones who had a right to be offended.

Pots and kettles are both black, my Grammie Dupree used to say, but only one is good for making tea. Yes, I know she mangled adages, twisting them into her brand of unique wisdom, but if you knew her like I did, you'd see this one made sense for the situation.

Called back to the stand, I was asked to describe, in great detail, the second most painful day of my life.

"Are you asking us to believe that Winston Durham, an attorney of good standing in the legal community, a man of integrity, was aware of these alleged forgeries?" Peterson injected pure disbelief into his tone. I indulged in a brief mental image of slapping his smarmy face. "It's a shame Mr. Durham isn't here to defend himself against such a base and vile accusation."

"Then maybe he shouldn't have thrown in with Reva McKinnon."

With that, I was excused from the stand.

I'm a redhead, which comes with a reputation for a fiery temper. Don't ask me why, I didn't make up the rules, and I can fire up with the best of them. When my fury burns, the fire is hot and fast and gone in a flare. It's when I turn cold with it that you have to watch out. Paul hadn't learned that one thing about me during our marriage, but now was as good a time as any.

When I finally did turn and level a look toward Thurston and Tippy Hastings, my face felt hard as a porcelain mask. For a second anyway, then it softened in surprise. Only Tippy looked my way, her forehead wrinkled, her eyes full of sorrow.

"I'm sorry." She mouthed at me, and I nearly fell off my seat.

Was it too little, too late? Absolutely. Did it take a bit of the fight out of me? Yeah, it did, but not all and not nearly enough to soften me toward the entire family, but I felt bolstered in learning she had a conscience. We'd never been mother and daughter to each other during my marriage to her son, but I'd thought we were friends. Then I'd thought we were enemies. Maybe we were neither, but it didn't matter anymore.

Lost in those types of thoughts, I missed it when the defense asked for a continuance, and the judge called a recess until Friday. Patrea had to drag me out of my seat when the judge exited to his chambers.

"Don't say anything, don't look at Paul, just walk out with your head held high," she spoke low enough only I could hear her. It sounded like a good idea to me, and so I did.

Despite my fears and misgivings, the trial hadn't been that bad.

"You were right. I was ready."

"Told you so."

Chapter Eleven

"There's one," Jacy practically shouted when she spotted an open parking space on our third trip past Blushing Bridal, the salon where we were already late for our first bridesmaid dress fitting. "Hurry up, or that guy in the Honda's gonna get it."

"All over it." Ignoring the blast of horns in her honor, Patrea shot across two lanes and whipped into the space just in time to shut the Honda out.

Neena made the sign of the cross and said, "Let me out of this death trap. Y'all drive like crazy people."

"Parking's a serious game on this side of town," Patrea clicked the locks and headed toward the salon at a clip. If the fitting ran long, we'd be late for the bridal shower Mrs. Heard had insisted upon planning, and since being late *ever* was on Patrea's list of things not to do, she was more on edge than usual.

"Check out this display." Jacy stopped in front of the window for a better look. Framed between a pair of ivory, lace curtains, a single armless, headless dress form turned away from the window to display the nipped-in waist and exquisite draping of an otherwise simple gown. Behind the dress, a dressing table with a tall mirror angled to show the front.

"It's nice." Neena agreed as she took Jacy's arm, pulled her along behind Patrea, who had already mounted the steps, and opened the salon door. "We could do something like that at Curated Collections."

"Understated, but eye-catching." I agreed.

"Ms. Heard," the woman who greeted us wore her hair in a perfectly smooth chignon that showed off the graceful curve of her neck. "My name is Sara; we spoke on the phone. If you would care to follow me, we have everything set up for you in the rose room."

"Nobody hopped to it like that when I picked out my bridesmaid dresses." Ten minutes later, Jacy—still breastfeeding—sipped sparkling cider while the rest of us drank champagne and watched the bridal salon staff do the dance of the pretty dresses. Or, in this case, the white garment bags and trays of snacks.

While Jacy's comment came off more amused than envious, Patrea sounded gruff—her typical response when embarrassed. "My mother probably made a call."

"I'll be sure to give her my regards," Neena grinned. "This is fun."

"Really?" But Patrea's shoulders relaxed slightly. "Okay, then. I think you'll like the dresses I've chosen. At least, I hope you will."

"I'm sure we will," Jacy said lightly. "You have excellent taste." She drained her cider and set the glass down. "Do you know, I think this room is bigger than my first apartment."

Several comfortable chairs faced a raised platform in front of floor-to-ceiling triple mirrors. To the seating area's right, double doors opened into a dressing room with even more chairs and curtained-off areas for privacy.

"You mean the one you tried to burn down with a hibachi?" I said.

"Hey, I figured the range hood would handle the smoke. I didn't realize the steaks would flame up like that."

Sara hung a long garment bag next to the four that were already there and surreptitiously checked the time on the narrow watch she wore with the face on the inside of her wrist.

"Shall we wait for the rest of your party, or would you like to begin now?"

Patrea sighed. "Go ahead. Taylor can't tell the difference between fashionably late and annoyingly so. At least now, I'll have an excuse if we don't make it to the shower in time."

"Taylor's your cousin, right?" I asked. "The one who works in finance?"

"The same," Patrea confirmed. "You'd think someone who spends all day staring at numbers would be better about watching the ones on the clock, but she's always been a bit of a flake."

"I'm sure you meant that in the nicest way possible," a voice piped up from behind us, in the direction of the entrance. "It's a good thing you're my favorite cousin, Patrea," the owner of the voice—presumably, Taylor herself—deadpanned.

I noted the family resemblance in dry humor rather than physical appearance because Taylor was Patrea's opposite in every way.

"It's about time," Patrea chided wryly but embraced her cousin with a grin.

"Ready?" Sara asked.

At Patrea's nod, Sara disappeared behind the mirrors and reappeared a moment later, pushing a dress form on wheels.

"Ooh," Neena's sigh summed up my own reaction perfectly.

Reminiscent of the 1920s and the color of the ocean on a clear morning, the dress featured beaded detail and a scalloped hemline that would fall, flatteringly, just below the knee.

The sight brought a sting of tears I quickly wiped away before turning to my friend. Jacy beat me to the punch, flinging her arms around the bride and nearly spilling Patrea's glass of champagne.

"That dress is everything," she practically shouted.

Patrea rolled her eyes. "You didn't think I'd put you in something truly hideous, did you?"

"You wouldn't be the first bride to get a kick out of humiliating her friends in an effort to ensure she's the best-dressed woman in the room," Taylor mused. "You ought to have seen the monstrosity my friend Cindi made me wear to her wedding. Lime green is not a color that fabric ought to be made out of—particular in satin and tulle."

"That just makes for ugly photos if you ask me," Patrea said, untangling herself from Jacy's grasp. "Now, let's get this show on the road."

We each chose a curtained cubicle and shimmied into our dresses. Patrea had little need to try on her own—I knew for a fact she'd been in for at least three fittings since she bought the dress even though it had fit her nearly perfectly right off the rack.

Though beautiful, the bridesmaid's dresses were a different story. The only one of us who managed to fill out her bodice was Jacy, who shimmied her girls and crowed, "Guess it's a good thing I still have my mom boobs."

In less than an hour, after being helped out of the dress to keep from ruining the tailor's marks, I already missed the feel of it on my body and almost hated putting back on the perfectly acceptable outfit I'd chosen to wear to the shower.

We arrived in front of Patrea's parents' house two minutes before we were scheduled to do so, thanks in large part to more erratic driving. White-knuckled and clutching the chicken handle, Neena shot me a fearful glance.

Personally, I felt that if we ran a contest, Jacy would take the prize for the bigger menace behind the wheel, but I decided to keep that opinion to myself.

The house looked exactly how I remembered, though I'd only seen it in passing. Two stories of classic red brick, white columns, and green shrubbery commanded several acres of sprawling, maple tree-dotted lawn. Focusing on the view of the lake in the distance, I could pretend my ex-husband's family didn't live nearby.

"Is that a tennis court out back?" Jacy squeaked with excitement. "And what's that other building over there? Is that an indoor pool?"

"If it is a pool, can I throw her in it if she doesn't shut up?" Neena gets cranky when she's afraid for her life.

Patrea bypassed the cavalcade of sleek sedans painted in neutral tones lining the circular driveway and parked facing the exit. "In case we need to make a speedy getaway," she said with a half-serious grin while the rest of us retrieved our gifts from the trunk.

"Don't gush over every little thing," Neena warned Jacy as we stepped into a nicely appointed foyer. Several polished tables graced the tile floors. On each rested a vase or bowl of artfully arranged flowers—mostly white and non-fragrant, of course, so as not to overwhelm the senses, or compete with whatever spectacular and appropriate hors d'ourves were sure to be served later.

A uniformed maid took our gifts before directing us into a large sunroom positioned at the back of the house—unnecessarily because this was Patrea's childhood home and she knew exactly where to find the party—where a half dozen round tables were all set for tea.

"I have to gush a little," Jacy ignored Neena's impatient sigh. "I feel like I've stepped into the pages of a magazine."

Spotting Patrea in the doorway, a horde of twittering socialites descended upon her, each demanding to see the ring while kissing the air around her head.

A woman, who looked absolutely nothing like Patrea except for they had the same eyes, introduced herself while her daughter was cheerfully engulfed.

"I'm Deanna Heard. It's a pleasure to meet you. Patrea speaks very highly of her new friends." She greeted us warmly.

"Pleased to meet you," Jacy said. "I have an aunt named Deanna. Everyone calls her Dottie. You have a lovely home." She subsided when Neena jabbed her with an elbow.

"Thank you for having us," I recognized Deanna from charity functions since she ran in the same circles as

Tippy Hastings, but we'd never been formally introduced. "We think very highly of Patrea, as well."

For the next hour, Neena, Jacy, and I watched Patrea get passed around from table to table, answering the same questions over and over. Her colors were cerulean and white. She and Chris planned to honeymoon, but not right away. She'd just opened her own law practice. Yes, she intended to take his name, and no, they hadn't decided when they might start a family. By the time poor Patrea managed to make her way to our table, it was time to open the gifts.

"I haven't had a bite to eat yet, and she's serving those crab puffs I love," Patrea sighed and looked hopefully in the direction of my plate.

"Here," I said, removing my napkin to reveal a hidden stash. "I saved you some."

Patrea shot me a grateful smile and inhaled three before being called away again.

"Bet we're not making toilet paper wedding dresses," Jacy muttered when Deanna called Patrea to the front to open gifts.

The first, an oval bowl with curved handles on either side and a matching plate in white with a pretty blue floral pattern, drew gasps of appreciation.

"That's an antique Meissen gravy boat," Jacy explained, "Blue onion print. I can't tell what year until I see the maker's mark."

The gifts alternated between fussy dinnerware and small appliances, except for Neena's—an oil painting of the Christmas tree farm in winter that drew a tear from Patrea.

"No," Jacy's protest rang out loud. "You probably shouldn't open that one right now."

But it was too late. Patrea had already peeled back white tissue paper to reveal screaming red underneath. As sexy sleepwear went, the slipdress-style with lace inserts, a plunging neckline, and crisscross straps was quite tasteful and far less scandalous than the gasped response it received from most of the assembled guests.

"It's La Perla." Jacy offered, her face nearly as red as the lycra nightie.

"I love it," Patrea's eyes gleamed, and she waggled her brows, "And so will Chris."

The party broke up shortly after, probably not because of Jacy's gift.

"I appreciate you letting me do this for you. I know this type of party isn't your style, but you've hardly let me do anything to help plan the wedding." Mrs. Heard murmured to Patrea as we made our exit.

Whoops.

"That was partly my fault, Deanna." None of us had given her a thought when we'd come up with the plan. "I've put on so many functions over the years that when Patrea told us she was getting married, I just went right into planning mode and didn't think. You should have been included, and I'm truly sorry."

"Well, what's done is done," Deanna said, but I sensed she'd put a black mark next to my name on her list.

Patrea intervened on my behalf. "We wanted a simple wedding, mother. Something a bit more intimate than the Ballantine. This was my choice to make, and I hope you can be happy for me."

"Don't be ridiculous, I'm thrilled for you, and Chris is a lovely man. Now, you call me if you need anything. Anything at all."

"You could help us plan our honeymoon."

"That sounds delightful, dear." Deanna kissed Patrea on the cheek, but I didn't think honeymoon planning made up for having no input on the wedding.

Chapter Twelve

After Patrea dropped me at home and I'd taken Molly out for a nice walk, I noticed we were almost out of dog food. When I pulled into the grocery store parking lot, it felt like an out-of-body experience. The place looked like a TV reporter should be on the scene asking people what had happened.

Men on ladders had already stripped off half the siding, all the signs were down, and barriers blocked all the spaces near the building. But since quite a few customers pushed loaded carts through the lot, I went ahead inside.

Outside changes paled in comparison to the mess I found when I did, but at least there was a sign letting me know why. Pardon Our Progress, it said. Progress was not the word I'd have used. Chaos would have been a more suitable and descriptive choice.

I wandered through aisles festooned with signs advertising a one-day sale with huge discounts, and everything must go. Most of everything had already gone—including Molly's preferred brand of dog food— and the store was still packed with people. Annoyed people, mostly, if their conversations were anything to go by.

By the time I made it halfway around the place, I'd heard that the former owners had recently sold the business because they were money-grubbing sellouts (in Mooselick River, that's a technical term) only interested in lining their pockets. Or they'd somehow been driven out by a competing group of money-grubbing retailers, which meant all the store brand merchandise would change. Prices were expected to skyrocket. The quality of the goods would go down the toilet. New management had laid off half the workers.

In other words, theories covered a broad mix of fact and fiction.

The only other topic people discussed obsessively concerned the recent series of tragic deaths.

"I heard they had to cut half of Margo Bodine's stomach out, and now they're waiting for a donor because she needs a transplant."

Was a stomach transplant even possible? I'd never heard of one, and I didn't recognize the voice coming from the next aisle, but Margo was a hot topic. Ernie had said her condition was serious but stable, so I thought it safe to discount some of the wilder variations on the theme of her impending death. It was probably a safe bet she hadn't died three times on the operating table or gone through every unit of blood the hospital had in stock.

But no one thought she would live, and maybe they were right.

I noticed a single bag of Molly's second favorite brand of kibble shoved way back on the bottom shelf and had bent to drag it out into the light when a wailing battering ram hit me on the backside and took me down. Purely by accident, my left foot shot out and returned the favor. I sprawled on the bag of dog food underneath my now-wailing assailant.

"Sorry." Even through her tears, I knew that voice. During my first job after I moved back to town, I'd worked with its owner, a singularly dull-witted young woman who now worked a cash register here and may or may not have just been fired by the possibly money-grubbing new store owners.

"Robin?" I asked.

She sniffed. "Yeah."

"Are you hurt?"

"I don't think so." She sounded miserable.

"Then would you mind getting off me?"

She did, but not with any grace or consideration. In fact, she placed a hand on the small of my back to push herself up.

"Ow," I said and dragged my sore body off the kibble and onto my hands and knees. "I'm okay, thanks for asking."

Robin didn't speak sarcasm.

"Oh, Everly. It's so awful," she squealed but didn't offer to help me up. I managed just fine on my own but barely made it to fully standing before she launched into my arms and nearly took us down again.

I looked around for someone to help, but the packed store—or at least this one aisle of it—had magically cleared.

"What's awful?" I figured I might as well ask since Robin had plastered herself onto me and wasn't letting go.

"I can't stand hearing them say such horrible things about her."

"You mean Margo Bodine?"

"No!" Her voice hit a pitch so high dogs were probably barking all over town. "Summer. Oh! How could they? She was my friend."

I heard ringing in my ears, my ribs hurt where she'd landed on them, and those weren't even the worst things that had happened to me all day. I wasn't getting the romaine I'd come here to buy or the dog food, I realized when I looked down, and the bag was gone.

But what the heck, I might as well cap off the day by listening to Robin's tale of friendship lost.

"I'm sorry for your loss." A trite phrase, to be sure, but one I sincerely meant. I even gave her a little pat on the back, which seemed to make matters worse. Robin sagged against me as if her bones had turned to rubber and wailed even harder.

I'd been the center of enough attention for one day, so I did the only thing that came to mind, and, grabbing my purse from the cart on my way past, half-dragged, half-supported her toward the door. A little fresh air might do us both some good.

Outside, she seemed to come back to herself a little, but not enough to be left alone. Besides, the wicked little voice in my head reminded me that she might have information to help Summer's case. I led her to the picnic table just off the edge of the parking lot, where the employees took their smoke breaks.

"Why don't you tell me about Summer? I think it will help you feel better."

"I still feel her, you know? She's all around me like an empty, aching hole, and it hurts. You know?"

I'd have never thought Robin would have such eloquence in her, but using just those few words, she'd described the way I felt when my beloved grandmother had passed. "I do. I truly am sorry."

"Then to have people call her a killer. How dare they? She wouldn't hurt anyone, even if they deserved it." The heat of anger began to dry Robin's tears. "You know what this means, don't you?"

If my life depended on it, I couldn't hazard a guess at what Robin would say. It's not nice, but based on my history with her, I always pictured the inside of her head to be like a hamster's bed—basically, a pile of fluff that moved a little every so often.

"If Summer didn't put poison in the food, then someone else did, and that means someone killed her, too. Like on purpose." While she talked, Robin dragged a long, red-tipped fingernail across the top of the table, making a cringe-worthy scraping sound.

"Do you have any idea who might want her dead?"

I might as well have been talking to the wind. "It's the only thing that makes sense," Robin said. "Especially after what she'd been through."

That last phrase sent a tingle of excitement through me. Finally, I might get information I could use. Except Robin didn't elaborate, so I felt compelled to ask. "You mean her divorce?"

"Well, sure. That was one thing."

"Was it bitter? Did she talk to you about her ex? What was the other thing?"

Robin's moment of lucid thought seemed to be over.

"I knew her. Like really knew her, you know? Like sisters or something. Do you have a sister? Then you know what I mean." She didn't even wait for me to answer. "Sisters tell each other everything. We were like that." She crossed her index and middle fingers, held them up as a symbol of hers and Summer's unity. "I don't know what I'm going to do without her."

And there went the waterworks again—and the high-pitched squealing cry. I really did think I heard a dog bark in the distance. "I know she never poisoned Frank Bodine. I bet that stupid wife of his did it and then killed Summer to cover her tracks. Or it could have been that horrid Mabel over at the diner. She's big and mean, and she wouldn't hire me when I needed a job. I think she's exactly the type to carry a grudge."

"What about Summer's ex-husband? Or maybe his new girlfriend?"

Rising, Robin rounded the table, drilled her pointy nail into my arm. "You're friends with killer Mabel. How do I know you weren't in on it? Are you trying to get on my good side, so I won't go to the cops?"

My mouth dropped open. Something that might have been a denial tried to pop out, but I think all I managed was a frustrated harrumph.

Eyes narrowed, Robin did the two-finger pointing thing between her and me. "I'm watching you."

"Uh, okay." What else could I say? Given a choice between talking to Robin and giving a cat a bath, I'd take the cat every time. Less painful and more productive.

"Don't mind Robin. She's a good person, but her porch light is stuck on dim," Summer shivered into view next to me. "Is everything okay between you and Mr. Pretty Pants?"

I so wanted to call Drew that when I saw him next.

"We're fine." I hoped I wasn't lying. "I probably should have told you about the way your emotions work when you don't exercise control. I know you weren't trying to hurt anyone."

Summer shrugged. "I really liked Frank Bodine. He was kind and thoughtful, and it was he who set up the Table at Home delivery. He liked to surprise Margo with a night off from cooking every so often."

"Then he picked the menu?"

"Sure."

I filed that fact away in case it became relevant later and then asked her the burning question of the day. "Can you tell me about you and Jack? Why did you get divorced?"

"Why does anyone get divorced?" She asked. "We weren't right for each other."

"I'll tell you about mine if you tell me about yours. No holds barred."

A moment passed while Summer contemplated the proposition. "Fine," she finally said, "you go first."

As succinctly as I could, I laid out my tale of woe. She let me get it all out without interrupting, and I thought maybe it was the first time anyone had done that for me. "I didn't realize how much control I'd given Paul because it happened over time and because it was a subtle thing, and all of his reasoning sounded, well, reasonable." I looked at her then, "You're a good listener. Now, it's your turn."

"I guess our stories aren't that much different," Summer mused. "If you don't count the money, the cheating, or the legal scandal."

"What does that leave?'

"Like I said, we realized we weren't right for each other, so we divorced. Amicably. And we remained friendly. That's all there was to it."

I'd have bet my pinky toe it wasn't, but if Summer didn't want to talk about it, I didn't see what I could do to make her.

"You can tell me the truth. I only want to help you."

"I am. There's no scandal, so you see, Jack didn't have any reason to murder me if that's what you're thinking. You need to look somewhere else because it wasn't Jack.'

With that, I had to be satisfied because a blink later, she was gone.

Chapter Thirteen

The last wooden crate filled with old milk bottles banged hard against my thighs as I lugged it toward the back door of Curated Collections. "Ugh," I muttered to no one. "That'll leave a mark."

Too bad the loan of David's truck hadn't come with the man himself. He'd have been able to carry two crates to my one. Then again, if I hadn't had this chore to finish, he'd have talked me into helping him do something equally as sweat-inducing at the old inn he'd been renovating all summer.

"That the last of them?" Neena held the back door open for me. "We finally hit a lull, and I was just coming to help."

"A likely story," I said. "Now that I've already done all the heavy lifting."

Neena looked fresh as a daisy, but then, she'd been inside the air-conditioned shop waiting on customers the entire time I spent unloading the truck.

"You've been busy today." The bottles rattled when I put the crate on the pile. I rested my fists against my lower back and bowed backward, trying to stretch the crick out of my spine. "I drove by earlier, on my way to show the apartment on Maple Street, and there were people outside waiting for you to open."

"Days like today, I wish we had a revolving door." Neena wasn't complaining, though. "Big news," she said. "Someone wants to commission me to do a mural on their barn wall. They're willing to pay a crazy amount of money."

I'd have hugged her if rivulets of sweat hadn't been chasing each other down my back. "That's incredible. Congratulations!"

"Don't get too excited," Neena said over her shoulder as I followed her toward the front of the shop. "I haven't said yes."

"Yet." Jacy chimed in. "But she's gonna."

"Of course, she is." I agreed.

Neena rounded on us, and it was then that I saw the worry on her face. "It's a wonderful opportunity. I'm not denyin' that, but do y'all have any idea how much work goes into something like a mural? I've never painted anything on that scale before." She began to tick off possible problems. "I have no idea how long it would take, or what to charge, and who's going to mind the shop while I'm off beautifyin' some barn halfway between here and Mackinaw?"

Jacy linked her arm with Neena's and practically dragged her partner toward a cluster of chairs for sale near the front window.

"Sit, and take a breath," she ordered, then went to the door and flipped the sign to closed for lunch. "I mean it. You're beginning to hyperventilate."

"I sure could use a drink." As much for Neena's benefit as my own, I went to the mini-fridge they kept in the office and grabbed both the sweet tea Neena preferred and the lemonade Jacy and I liked best. Even with the air conditioners running, beads of water condensed on the outside of all three glasses as I carried them back to where Neena looked calmer already.

She guzzled half the glass of tea in one go. "Thanks, I needed that."

"Now, as far as your mural goes. If you want the job, you take it." I settled next to her, put my hand on her arm in a show of support. "You know I'm always happy to pitch in here, and so will Leandra. She always loves the chance to sit and gossip with the customers. Plus, she's not bad at talking people into buying those extra little things she thinks they might like."

Our attempts to alleviate Neena's worries appeared to have the opposite effect.

"Then there's the mechanics of it all. I'd need ladders and bigger brushes. Where am I going to get ladders? Hudson hired out anything that required climbing. He didn't like heights."

"Or," I remembered some of the work David had been doing on the exterior of the inn, "David has a set of staging, and I know he'll be finished with it as soon as he gets the copper roof panels installed on the cupola. He had to have them custom-made, and it took a week longer than he expected, but they came in yesterday, so he'll get them up soon enough."

Gesturing toward Neena with her glass of lemonade, Jacy said, "The way you two were sparking the other night, I bet he'd loan you the staging and offer to hold your brushes while you paint."

Jacy hadn't meant the comment as a double entendre, but it still made Neena blush.

"I have no idea what y'all are talking about."

A conspiratorial grin spread over my face, and I leaned over to look past Neena and exchange same with Jacy. "So, it wasn't just me who saw them?"

"Oh no," Jacy shook her head, a twinkle lighting in her eyes. "There was definite sparkage going on. The man looked like he'd been hit by lightning when you walked off that dance floor."

A little over a month past the first anniversary of her husband's murder, Neena still hadn't put herself back on the market, and I didn't think she should until she was ready. But I also didn't want her to be lonely or to say no to the possibility simply because she'd formed the habit of being alone. I studied her face for signs of dismay or pain but saw hints of neither.

"So long," Neena said, "as we didn't make a spectacle of ourselves, I guess I can live with that."

"Does that mean what I think it means?" Jacy got up to flip the closed sign to open but held off until Neena answered.

"It means it felt nice to be held by a man."

I found myself in an awkward position between two friends who were just beginning to think about dating. Both had ghosts in their past—in Neena's case, I mean that literally since her husband had been the first to haunt me. I didn't want to see either of them get hurt, even if I thought it was time both of them moved on.

"Any man?" I asked. "Or David in particular."

To her credit, Neena thought carefully before she answered, and that alone was enough to set my mind at ease.

"David. Definitely David. There's something about him that touches me."

Jacy opened her mouth to, I'm sure, make an inappropriate comment about David touching Neena but shut it again when the shop door opened.

"Hey, Mrs. Dexter. I've got your books in the back. I'll go get them," Jacy said instead.

Barbara Dexter, friend to my mother and owner of the Bide-A-Way Motel, enjoyed a juicy tidbit of gossip as much as the steamy romance novels Jacy always put aside for her.

Settling the box of books on one hip, Barb scored herself a twofer for the day. "Darned shame about Frank Bodine, isn't it? Hemlock is an ugly way to die, but I suppose we can be thankful he went sudden-like. Hard on those who are left behind when there's no time to prepare."

As much as the topic of dead husbands might bother Neena, her voice stayed soft, and even when she said, "I suppose we're all selfish enough to wish we had more time to say goodbye, but no matter how much, it wouldn't be enough."

Nodding, Barbara patted Neena's arm, "And then that poor Merryfield girl." She made that tsking sound with teeth and tongue. "They say it was all her fault, too. You know I heard her ex-husband already moved back into the house, and they haven't even had the funeral yet. Must have a set of brass ones on him."

I did not want to discuss Jack's brass whatevers, but since Barb always seemed dialed in, it couldn't hurt to pry a little deeper. She might know something that would help me solve Summer's murder. Unfortunately, she didn't know anything more about Jack, so I turned to another topic.

"Is there any word on Margo's condition? I stopped in at the grocery store yesterday afternoon, and people were talking. They had her at death's door."

Twisting her lips to one side, Barbara made a harrumphing sound. "Margo Bodine could've gone down with the Titanic and still made it out alive. She has the luck of the devil himself."

Presumably, that meant she'd survived. It also seemed as if she wasn't one of Barbara's favorite people. In a town as small as Mooselick River, everyone knows everyone, and as the saying goes, familiarity breeds contempt. Petty grievances spring up like weeds and get tended like prize roses.

"She did lose her husband. I'd call that pretty unlucky," Jacy chided gently.

"Suppose so, but she's home and no worse for the wear. I heard," Barbara leaned in and lowered her voice, a sign she was about to say something particularly juicy. "She's made an appointment with that new lady lawyer to file a lawsuit against Summer's business insurance. Wrongful death on behalf of Frank, and reckless endangerment for herself."

My brows shot up. "Do you know—" Before I could pry deeper, the shop door opened to admit two chattering women I didn't recognize. Probably tourists. By the time they'd left, Barbara had also gone leaving me almost wishing there was some sort of town function afoot so I could hit Martha up for information.

Almost.

Chapter Fourteen

"Where are you?"

"What? I don't even get a hello?"

"Hello," Patrea's voice sounded dry over the phone. "Where are you?"

"I'm at Leo's office doing a lease for the apartment on Maple. Why?"

"Stay there, I'm on my way."

She hung up, and I worried until she pulled in next to my—technically Leo Hansen's—new tenant's beat-up Volvo just as I finished putting a copy of the lease in their welcome packet.

"Inside, you'll find a card with my number and also a refrigerator magnet. Call me if you need anything, night or day. I've also added menus from the local takeout places and a sheet with other useful phone numbers. There's also a map of the town with all of the businesses and municipal buildings marked. Welcome to Mooselick River."

I went through my typical spiel with the nice couple, but most of my attention focused on watching Patrea's mood as she got out of her car.

"Oh, and if you order pizza from Bertino's, make sure to tell them you want the special sauce. It's a local secret, and you have to ask for it, but it's the best."

The Lancasters went out as Patrea came in.

"Everything okay?" I asked.

"Sure." She didn't seem upset. "You're done for the day, right? There are wedding-related errands that require your vast and impressive organizational skills."

Done for the day was a relative term since it was not even nine-thirty in the morning. I managed all of Leo's rental properties, but he kept them maintained so meticulously that even though I was on call twenty-four hours a day, my job took almost none of my time. As long as I had my cell phone handy in case of a tenant emergency, I didn't have to hang around the office all day.

Leo paid me pretty well, and my expenses were low, so it was the ideal job—a statement I will deny I made when a tenant moves out and leaves the place a mess, or I'm crawling through cobwebs to heat up frozen pipes in the winter.

"You don't have to lay it on quite so thick. I've got time for wedding errands," I smiled because she did and noted that it was the sort of activity that happened a lot more often these days, so I said, "You're happy."

"I am," Patrea said, "and I'll be even happier once all this stuff is nailed down. Our first stop is the Blue Moon."

I stopped in the middle of slinging my purse strap over my shoulder and gave her a look. "And now I know why you're dragging me along. It has nothing to do with my organizational skills. You think Mabel's mad at you for hiring Summer, and you want me to be your buffer when you go talk to her."

"Don't be ridiculous. You're my Maid of Honor, and it's your duty to—" Her eyes looked everywhere but at me.

"Yeah, yeah. Go sell that steaming pile to someone who'll buy it," I said lightly. "You're scared of Mabel."

"Fine," she reluctantly admitted. "I'm scared of Mabel. Do you feel better now you made me say it?"

I followed her out the door, locking it behind me as I left.

"You know," I said, not earning myself any points. "I think I do."

We got into her car, leaving mine where it was for the time being. "Have you seen her, though? She looks like she could lift a car up and change a tire without a jack."

The town scrolled past my window as we drove through. "I know, but under all that bluff and bluster, she's a pussycat."

"So are tigers, but you won't see me poking one of those in the snout, either."

The image of Patrea poking Mabel anywhere made me giggle. "I think you'll get along better with her if you avoid that particular activity."

"I'm beginning to regret letting you go with me today. You're enjoying my discomfort way too much."

Letting me go? Letting? Puhlease.

"What else is on the agenda for this day of wedding planning fun?"

"Flowers. Chris loved your idea for the potted trees, by the way. But he's leaving the flower selections up to me. Do you have any idea what a tussie-mussie might be?"

"Sure." I grinned at her skeptical tone. "It's a Victorian-style bouquet carried in a metal holder or vase."

Patrea sniffed. "Just the name of it sounds undignified. And fussy. Tussie-mussie fussy. Gah. Why would I ever want one?"

"You might be surprised. Some of the holders are really understated, and the effect can be elegant if you choose the right flowers."

We'd pulled into the diner parking lot, but Patrea made no move to get out of the car. Instead, she tapped her index and middle fingers in rhythm on the steering wheel.

"What are you doing?"

"Playing eeny meeny miny mo."

"Why are you playing eeny meeny miny mo?" I gentled my voice the way you do with cornered animals. This wasn't the Patrea I knew.

"Just trying to decide if I should brave Mabel or call a travel agent and book plane tickets to Vegas."

I swallowed a laugh. "And how's that working out for you?"

"Mabel's winning, but I'm thinking I'll have a better shot if I go three out of five."

"You could always," I suggested, "go with the platinum resort wedding package in Hackinaw."

Patrea sighed. "Chris would hate that even more than he'd hate Vegas. I vote we do the florist. First, it'll give me time to build up my courage."

The florist meant The Delightful Daisy, which was the only option in town. Or technically, the only option in a three-town radius since Riverside Floral had closed the year I graduated from high school. The owners of the Daisy managed to keep the doors open by adding a set of greenhouses and branching out with a line of garden supplies and lawn ornaments.

Splashes of floral color surrounded a rustic, three-sided farm stand I intended to visit before we left. More flowers rioted around the greenhouse doors and in pots scattered across trestle-style tables, dripped from baskets hung on homemade racks. Several bright flags flapped in the light breeze and lined a path leading around the back of the building that I couldn't wait to explore.

"I think I'll buy three of those hanging baskets for my front porch. The pink ones are so cheerful, and look over there," I said, pointing toward a pair of white, fluted pots with snow-white hydrangeas trained up some sort of frame to look like small trees. "Those would be perfect at the ends of the aisle for the wedding."

Patrea looked and nodded. "They would. We'll add them to the list, but first, let's get the bouquet and table centerpieces out of the way."

I followed her across the small parking lot and into the shop, where the florist was already talking to a customer. Patrea's phone rang just as we walked in, so she took it outside, leaving me alone in the shop. While I waited, I browsed the shelves of gift options and shamelessly eavesdropped. It wasn't all that difficult since the woman ordering flowers didn't make any attempt to keep her voice down.

"I'll need something to frame the urn. It has to be roses, but yellow ones, not red. Frank always preferred yellow roses."

Frank. As in Frank Bodine? Assuming she must be the unsinkable Margo Bodine, I angled my way between the shelves to get a better look at the woman at the counter. Unsuccessfully, as it turned out.

All I managed to garner were vague impressions of a tall woman with dark hair and pale skin—possibly from her recent illness—wearing a white sundress with a printed silk scarf around her neck even in the heat of summer.

Just as I got into position, Margo—I did confirm that much when the florist mentioned her name— completed her business, turned away from me, and passed Patrea on her way back in.

"We have another errand after this one," Patrea said briefly to me on her way past. "I'm Patrea Heard. We spoke on the phone."

"Delia James. You're marrying Chris Evergreen."

Patrea inclined her head. "I am." A smile played around the corners of her mouth.

"Congratulations on getting him to commit. Many have tried, and many have failed." If not for her good-natured grin, I'd have found Delia's comment a bit off-putting. Still, she seemed to know her flowers, and we spent the next little while browsing through notebooks with photos of her past work.

"You're very talented," I said, eliciting a smile in return.

"What I am," said Delia, "is lucky. Flowers are my passion. Not everyone gets paid for doing what feels like play."

Her words gave me pause. I'd been working for Leo for a year, and it was a good job. A convenient job most of the time, but it wasn't my passion by any stretch. Was I missing out on something by just going with the flow? I'd have to think about the direction my life was taking, but later. This was Patrea's moment.

Except she wasn't taking advantage of it. "I had no idea there would be so many options." Patrea put one notebook down and took up another. It was the third time she'd leafed through each one. "I'm not sure."

Delia's smile had gone slightly wooden. We'd been there longer, I thought, than she expected, and Patrea wasn't any closer to a decision than when she started. "Do you have a picture of the dress? Maybe if I could see it, I could give you some constructive advice."

Looking chagrined, Patrea admitted, "I don't."

"Well, maybe you could describe the dress."

"It's sort of a cream color, and it's long." Patrea was out of her depth, so I stepped in.

"It's a twenties-inspired, hand-beaded ivory sheath, with capped sleeves and a stylized bodice. Nipped-in waist, flared at the knees, with a short train."

"Veil?" Delia asked.

I shook my head. "Would ruin the lines of the dress."

"I've got just the thing. Wait here." Delia disappeared into the back room and returned moments later carrying a horn-shaped vase made of blue glass and metal fluted in geometric lines. "This just came in yesterday with some other samples, and I think it would make the perfect tussie-mussie holder for that dress."

She might hate the word, but Patrea's eyes lit up, and when Delia passed her the vase, she cradled it in her hands. "This will be perfect with white petunias to mimic the shape and contrast against the glass. Is there any way you can get it in... what was it again?" She looked at me.

"Cerulean," I supplied.

Delia consulted her catalog and confirmed the shade as an option. From there, the centerpieces fell into place as the same company supplied multiple types of vases in the same color that would look fantastic, filled with petunias and some spiky greens. Delia set up the dates for delivery and totaled the bill, adding the two hydrangea arrangements we'd seen outside.

Patrea opted to pay in full rather than just give a deposit.

"Was that Margo Bodine who was here earlier?" Once our business was done, I fished for information.

"It was," Delia confirmed as she selected several delicate blue flowers with long stalks spearing up from buckets in the cooler behind the counter. "Such a shame about Frank. I'll miss his smile."

"Did you know him well?"

Several moments passed in silence while Delia leaned down to find a pair of snips. "He came in every week to buy flowers for his wife." The snips went snicker-snack as she took off several inches from the bottom of each stem. When she had them at the length she wanted, she went back to the cooler for a selection of yellow roses.

"I've been doing this a few years now, and I can count on one hand the men who do that type of thing. It takes a level of devotion, but Frank was a romantic. It's an honor to make the floral arrangements for his funeral."

"And Margo?"

"No idea. Today was the first day I ever met the woman." Finished with the yellow rose stems, Delia gathered both colors into one bundle and dropped them into a smaller, water-filled container. "She wasn't what I expected, though."

I'd have liked to learn why, but Patrea announced it was time to leave, and Delia seemed relieved. I assumed she had a lot of work to do with two funerals.

"Are you doing the flowers for Summer Merryfield's funeral as well?"

At the mention of Summer's name, Delia's face set into disapproving lines. "I'm not." But she didn't elaborate.

Back in the car, I wondered out loud. "Do you think she didn't want to do Summer's flowers, or maybe she wasn't asked?"

"I don't know," Patrea said, turning the key in the ignition, "but you can probably talk to her ex about it if you want to be nosy. That's what that call was about. He's our next stop."

"Really? Why?"

"He wanted to return my deposit check. I told him he could just tear it up, but he insisted it had to be returned in person because Summer would have wanted it that way. I figured you wouldn't mind the chance to snoop."

"You figured right. Something's off with this whole accidental poisoning scenario, but I don't have enough information to pin down what it is."

Chapter Fifteen

"Do you want me to handle this so you can keep your distance? Professionally, I mean," I asked on the way over to talk to Jack Merryfield.

Patrea took her eyes off the road long enough for her tires to come dangerously close to the yellow line. "What professional distance?"

"Aren't you suing Summer's estate on behalf of Margo Bodine?" I knew as soon as the words passed my lips, I'd been bamboozled by Barbara Dexter. "Never mind. I should have known better."

"Well, I should think so. Even if she had come to me and asked me if I thought she had a case, I wouldn't feel right taking her on as a client."

"But you think she has a case?"

A moment passed before Patrea let out a gusty sigh. "People sue for more reasons than just money."

It wasn't an answer, but I thought I knew what she was trying to say, and it actually made me feel a little better about Margo Bodine to believe she might be so broken-hearted at the loss of her husband, she wanted to lash out at someone. I'd let Barbara cloud my thinking about a woman I'd never met.

"This is the place."

Summer had lived in a modest salt-box house plopped on at least an acre of land right on the edge of where the more populated part of town nudged up against the surrounding country.

"Looks like Jacy's mom had a hand in the landscaping," I said, and then explained in more detail when I realized Patrea probably hadn't a clue what I meant. "Leandra's thumbs are green right down to the bone, and her place looks a lot like this."

Walkways of paving stones set into close-cropped grass made pretty patterns as they wound around and through various types of planting beds—some raised mounds of soil, some held in by timber frames, some with arched half-hoops marching along them. Beans climbed a set of strings attached to one side of a long pergola while thumb-sized cucumbers dripped beneath chicken-wire frames tilted against the other side.

Flower petals, lush herbs, and freshly turned earth loaned their scents to air that hummed with the sounds of bees busy at their work of gathering and spreading pollen from one flower to the next. Tiny nozzles sprouted from a network of black tubing, spraying or dripping water to soak into thirsty roots.

"It's like an oasis of peace," Patrea whispered since the beauty seemed to call for that level of reverence.

I couldn't disagree with her, and you can brand me fanciful, but I also felt a sadness there, as if the garden mourned its keeper.

The door opened before we mounted the front steps.

"Thank you for coming," Jack Merryfield swayed gently on his feet as he stood in the doorway. The skin around them was red and puffy, but his eyes looked clear enough that I amended my first impression of him. He wasn't drunk, but he didn't look well.

"Of course," Patrea said. "And I'm sorry to bother you during this sad time. It really would have been fine if you'd simply torn up the check. Or I could have called the bank to stop payment if that would have set your mind at ease."

"No, it's better this way. This is one of the last things I can do for Summer. Now, if you'd just wait here, I'll be right back—"

"We're sorry for your loss, Mr. Merryfield, and we don't want to intrude, but would it be okay if we came in for a moment," I spoke up. "I hate to ask, but I was hoping I could use your bathroom. We've been out all day running errands, you see." Anything to get my foot—and the rest of me—in the door.

For a moment, I thought he was leaning toward saying no, but then Jack stepped back and gestured for us to come inside. I wished Summer would show up to give me the guided tour, but she didn't, and I supposed I didn't blame her for that. It probably wouldn't have been easy for her if she'd been the victim of spousal abuse.

"It's right down the hall," Jack gestured. "Second door on the left."

I didn't need to go, but since I was there, I made use of the facilities and then washed up in the small sink. Without so much as a shred of remorse, I swung open the medicine cabinet door. I don't know what I expected to find, but it seemed like the thing to do.

Fully half the contents were bottles carrying Momma Wade's label—from cramp relief to wart remover. Somehow, I doubted Jack's fiancé had stocked these shelves. Peggy struck me as the type to go for brand names—most likely brands recommended in the pages of women's magazines, not home-brewed remedies.

Wouldn't she have cleared out Summer's things to make room for her own? Something seemed off.

"Summer," I hissed. "Can you hear me?" No answer

Nothing looked out of place, but how would I know for sure? Jack could have added the hemlock to any one of these bottles at any time and then waited for Summer to die the next time she had cramps or a headache. He didn't live here anymore, so no one would ever suspect him—the perfect alibi.

Long moments passed while a series of what-ifs played through my head. What if, for instance, Summer had called Jack or vice versa? Maybe they argued over something to do with the divorce or the house, or whatever.

Maybe she told him she was headed out to deliver Frank and Margo their Meal at Home or whatever it was, but she had a headache. He could have urged her to stop at home and use the remedy he'd poisoned.

According to what I'd read on the Internet, death from hemlock poisoning could take several hours, depending on the amount ingested.

I pictured Summer rushing in, grabbing the brown bottle and downing a dose. She probably hadn't eaten anything other than taste-testing her dishes, so she wouldn't be surprised when she began to feel a little queasy. She'd have held her stomach as she walked out the door but ignored the symptoms because she had a job to do.

She could have told her ex her plan to stop in town and do some prep for Patrea's tasting the next day.

All Jack had to do was show up at the café, and wait to make sure she was down for the count, and then...well, what about Frank?

Or, what if he'd put the poison in a bottle of extract she kept at home? Maybe she'd run out of something at the café, zipped home for the one she had in her pantry, and gone back to season a dish with death.

In a third option, Jack showed up at the café with a poison-spiked beverage, then offered to help Summer with her delivery. He could have slipped the poison into the Bodine's food to cover his tracks. Any one of those could play.

Patrea could be alone in a room with a killer right this minute. I left the bathroom and hurried back to watch over her.

"Can I call someone for you?" I heard Patrea ask as I walked back down the hall. She sounded flustered.

"No, there's no one." Jack's voice sounded husky. What had happened while I was in the bathroom? I hadn't been gone five minutes.

I stepped into the living room to see Patrea standing next to Jack as he sat on a chair upholstered in a pretty, striped fabric, his head in his hands, his shoulders shaking. When she saw me, Patrea widened her eyes and shook her head as if to say she didn't know what had happened to bring him to tears.

"Is everything okay?" I asked.

"Nothing will ever be okay again," Jack wailed. "Summer is gone, and now I'll never get the chance to make things right with her."

If Jack was innocent, the next time I saw Summer, I needed to ask if her husband had always been this emotional or if it was only death that brought out the drama. Maybe I wouldn't put it in such bald terms. I wouldn't want to sound callous.

"Let me get you something to drink," Patrea abandoned me and headed to the kitchen where I heard her opening cabinet doors, then the clinking of one glass against another.

Meanwhile, Jack sat in pretty much the same position as he'd been since I came into the room. Seeing him rubbing his temples gave me an awful idea.

"Do you have a headache? Let me get you something for that. Is it okay if I look in your medicine cabinet?" I watched him to gauge his reaction, and he never so much as flinched. Probably got rid of the evidence the minute he heard Summer was gone.

"I took something already," he began to tip his face up, and it occurred that I had him at a disadvantage. He had no idea I was onto him, so maybe he'd give something away. I schooled my expression into one of concern and made sure I'd done a convincing job of it by the time his eyes met mine. "But there's no remedy for regret."

Or for a guilty conscience.

Except he didn't look guilty so much as he just looked miserable, but I'd been fooled by a killer with good acting skills once already.

"What did you do to—"

"What do you regret, Jack?" Patrea pinned me with a look that said I should let her handle him as she spoke loud enough to drown me out. All sympathy and gentleness, she handed him the glass of ice water and urged him to share. "If you get it off your chest, you'll feel better. I promise."

Jack wanted to talk. I could all but feel the need to confess rising up in him. Patrea yanked me down onto the sofa next to her so I wouldn't keep looming over him while we waited to hear what he had to say.

"I knew something like this would happen one day, and I didn't put a stop to it."

Finally, something interesting. "Go on," I urged.

"What did she know about cooking professionally? There are rules and regulations for these things. You can't just rent a restaurant and call yourself a chef. That's not how it works."

"How does it work?" I had to ask.

"A woman like Summer needs a strong hand," he said, his choice of words putting my hackles up. "Needed."

"In what way?" Patrea asked, her back going rigid.

"She was reckless." He said, his voice sounding wooden. "Impulsive. Always coming up with some new idea, something else to try, and she was never happy with what she already had. This need for more, it came between us. I thought if I left, she'd see how chasing all these foolish notions wasn't worth the cost."

"I guess that plan backfired on you. What happened next?" I said and shot a quelling look at Patrea. I know her well enough to know when she's close to going off on someone, and without hardly trying, he'd pushed her close to the line.

What a pathetic little man.

"She wouldn't take me back."

"Maybe you'll have better luck with Peggy. She doesn't seem to have any serious aspirations beyond upgrading to the platinum wedding package."

I couldn't help it, I snapped at him. Better than slapping him. Not as satisfying.

"Thank you for coming. I think I'd like to be alone now. I need to learn how to live without the person who always helps me through traumatic situations."

"But…" I stopped when Patrea jabbed her elbow into my side and fell into a sullen silence while she offered our condolences, then followed her out to the car.

"What did you do that for?" I demanded. "I still think he knows something."

"If he kept talking, one of us might have needed bail money. Just leave it alone, and be thankful Summer got away from him and at least had a small taste of the life she wanted."

I guessed she was right.

Chapter Sixteen

When we walked into the Blue Moon, tension hung like smoke in the air. A muted hush replaced the usual buzz of conversation. Every eye in the place followed the same track from plate to corner booth where Ernie Polk and diner owner Mabel glared at each other across brightly colored Formica.

Jacy crooked a finger at us from the booth in the far corner, and we wove through tables as quietly as we could to join her.

"What's going on?" I whispered because the situation seemed to demand it.

"Ernie and Mabel are in a fight," she hissed unhelpfully and moved over so I could sit facing the scene of interest, which left an annoyed Patrea to take the spot facing away. Trying to look casual about it, she slid all the way in and spun to rest her back against the wall so she could see what was happening.

"I can see that well enough. What about?"

"Summer Merryfield."

"What'll it be?" Thea Lombardi's voice sounded foghorn loud against the unnatural quiet.

"Pastrami on wheat, with swiss, extra tomatoes, and both mustard and mayo. And a side of onion rings."

As usual, Thea quirked an eyebrow and let her gaze track down toward my hips in silent rebuke. Like she was anyone to talk given the size of her caboose.

"Tuna melt with fries and an iced tea," Patrea chose.

"Two iced teas," I added.

"And make those rings a large with extra sauce," Jacy chimed in.

Meanwhile, Mabel crossed her arms over her chest and did her level best to stare a hole through Ernie's forehead while he mirrored her posture and expression. Built like a linebacker, I'd put my money on Mabel if an actual fight broke out.

All across the diner, people poked at their food and nursed cold cups of coffee for as long as possible. No one wanted to miss the action. Not that the current staring contest constituted action, exactly, but Mabel was known for her temper.

Anyone who knew her well also found her to be a generous person who championed underdogs, but you had to get past the prickly exterior to see the mushy heart inside.

The silent war dragged uncomfortably on—to the point where I began to feel as if I should do or say something. The way most of the patrons had begun to fidget made me think I wasn't the only one feeling like I stood on the edge of a volcano that was bound to erupt.

The only person in the place who seemed unaware of the rising tension was Thea. She slapped my plate down on the table with a cracking sound that made at least two people jump, then did the same with the rest of our order.

"Getcha anything else?'

I shook my head. Mabel never flinched. Ernie might have been carved in stone. The whole situation tipped over the edge into ridiculous.

Still, not a single patron left. Not even when Thea went from table to table, slapping bills face down on each one.

Finally, without turning her head or dropping eye contact, Mabel barked, "Thea!"

In no hurry, Thea ambled over.

"Yeah, boss?"

"Did I put poison in the potatoes you dropped off at Merry Eats the other night?"

"No, boss."

"Did I try to put Summer Merryfield out of business?"

"No, boss."

"Did I tell you to lie to Ernie Polk for me?"

"No, boss."

Mabel rose from her seat, picked up the check Thea had placed next to Ernie's plate, crumpled it in her hand, and tossed it into his coffee. "Food's on the house." Spinning on one heel with more grace than a woman of her stature might be expected to have, Mabel made her way back to the kitchen, each footstep sounding like thunder.

And still, no one moved.

Not until Ernie slid out of the booth and stalked toward the exit. He turned once, pinned me with a look, then went through the door, careful not to let it slam behind him.

"Thanks for the tip," Thea didn't hide her disgust, and suddenly the place filled with the rustle of movement and a steady hum of low conversation.

"Show's over," I said to Jacy and dragged an onion ring through the dipping sauce. At least Mabel's rings were just as good cold as hot.

Pan lids clanged from the kitchen, the cash register dinged cheerfully as people lined up to pay their bills, and it didn't take long for the place to clear out.

Ten minutes later, Mabel stuck her head out of the kitchen and, seeing there was no one left besides Jacy, Patrea, and me, joined us.

"Thea," she raised her voice slightly as she settled beside me in the booth. "Plate up four pieces of apple pie, then go on your break."

We watched Thea do exactly that. Plate up the pie, but not deliver it to the table. She collected a pack of cigarettes from somewhere under the counter and left without a backward glance.

I got up to retrieve the pie.

"That woman is dumber than a bucket of horse manure." Mabel might have been saying the sky was blue for all the emphasis she used, but her movements were sharp when she sliced her fork through crust and succulent apple slices drenched in cinnamon-scented filling.

Our napkin holder was empty, so I went behind the counter for a few extras, and Jacy being who she was, got up, grabbed a can of whipped cream from the cooler, came back, and shot a liberal cloud of white on top of Mabel's pie.

"You want?" She gestured the can toward mine, but I shook my head.

"I didn't kill Summer Merryfield." Mabel used the same amount of inflection as she had when pronouncing Thea an idiot. It was a statement of fact, not a defense or attempt to convince.

"Of course, you didn't." Jacy's hand slid across the table to give Mabel's a gentle squeeze. "I can't begin to understand what Ernie was thinking."

He was thinking Mabel might have wanted to do away with her competition. If I didn't know better, I might have thought the same, and I said as much, earning myself a hot look from Jacy but a nod from Mabel.

"There's a certain amount of logic to the theory," I waved my fork to emphasize the point. "Professional jealousy's as good a motive as any other. Not that I think you poisoned anyone." I ate another bite of pie. "You're more of a hands-on kind of person. You'd do your killing up close and personal."

It isn't easy to chew pie with your foot in your mouth.

"That sounded…" I tried to backtrack, but Mabel only let out a chortle.

"Damn skippy," she said. But the mood had lightened. Mabel added more whipped cream to the half-slice of pie she had left. "I didn't kill Summer."

"We know," Jacy echoed my thoughts on the subject as she followed suit with the can of cream, again offering it to me when she was done.

Again, I declined. I'm a purist when it comes to apple pie. Good apple pie—and this was good pie—doesn't need anything else to detract from the flavor. Chocolate pie is another story. You can disagree with me all you like; I respect everyone's pie choices equally.

The slam of the back door signaled the end of Thea's smoke break. Jacy watched her half-hearted attempt at cleaning tables for only a few moments before rolling her eyes, getting up, and grabbing the dirty rag out of the other woman's hand.

"You're doing it all wrong."

It was a day for drama. Thea snatched the rag back.

"Don't tell me what to do! You don't work here anymore."

"Work being the operative word in that sentence." Jacy made another grab for the rag. Thea held on, and the resulting tussle ended with each of them holding half a torn piece of material.

"Shouldn't you do something?" I asked Mabel, who shook her head and then picked up the dropped thread of our earlier conversation.

"I'm not as dumb as I look," she said. "Vinnie De Luca was in here last night handing out a lecture on the evils of foraging for wild edibles. That's how he put it...wild edibles."

I nodded because I'd heard the wind-up to that particular talk already.

"But I knew Summer pretty well, and I'd lay dollars to donuts she never made a mistake like that."

"She's right." Summer's head popped up over the edge of the booth behind Mabel. "Don't let her gruff manner fool you. Mabel helped me out a lot when I was just getting started with the café."

"Of course." I really hate carrying on two conversations at once, and where had she been earlier when I needed her?

"Then, here comes Ernie Polk asking me how I felt about having another restaurant open in town and was Summer cutting into my business." Mabel slapped a hand down on the table. "Did it look like I was hurting for customers? The place was packed when he came wandering in here with his stupid face and his stupid questions."

"I'd have hired that girl on the spot if she'd been looking for a job. I owed her that much after what—" As if catching herself in the act of offering too much information, Mabel paused and amended the end of her sentence. "She turned me down."

"She would have let me add my own ideas to the menu. It would have been like a partnership in a way." Summer assured. "But I wanted to strike out on my own. I wanted something that was mine alone. And when I told her that, did she get mad? Nope. She offered to loan me the money to open my place."

That was new and interesting information.

"Did you tell Ernie what you've just told me?"

"'Course not." Mabel put on her stubborn face. It looked a lot like her regular face. "If he wants information from me, he ought not to come in here swinging that badge around like it was his—"

"Let go!" Thea shrieked and drew my attention.

In all the years I've known her, I'd only seen three people push Jacy past her breaking point, and they'd all been related to her by blood.

For all her size, Mabel was up and across the diner before my butt managed to clear the fake leather seat. She stepped between the two spitting women just as the squeeze bottle of ketchup they were fighting over went off—right in her face.

A drop of ketchup slid down Mabel's chin, quivered there for a second, then hit the floor with a splat that sounded loud in the sudden silence. No one moved. No one spoke. It was like looking at statues in a garden.

Jacy broke first. Even though she curled her lips under and pressed down with her teeth to hold it back, the laugh snorted out her nose. It sounded funny, so I laughed. I'm sorry, but that's my excuse, and I'm sticking to it.

Then I caught sight of Thea's face, the habitual expression of bored indifference replaced by one of fear—sparked, I was sure, by the combination of ticking off a former roller derby queen and her job being on the line. That lasted about three seconds, which was as long as it took for Mabel to snatch up the ketchup bottle and take aim.

I figured Mabel had earned the moment of catharsis after having to deal with Thea for nearly a year, and I might have let out a cheer, but Mabel still had the bottle in her hand, and I didn't want to be next.

Thea's face took the full shot. She clenched her teeth and stood there, spine stiff and fists clenched until Mabel took pity on her.

"Get yourself cleaned up, and then go home." Mabel's mouth twitched, but she kept a stern look.

"But my shift doesn't end for another two hours, and you know I need—" Her voice thick with tears, Thea protested. "I'll clean up the mess, and I'll do better."

In the gentlest tone I had ever heard her use, Mabel let Thea off the hook, "It's okay, Thea. I'll pay you for the hours you missed. You run along, now, and I'll see you in the morning."

Visibly relieved, Thea did as she was told.

When she'd gone, Mabel said, "Now, the people who laughed--"

"Sorry," I said without a shred of remorse. "But you should have seen the look on your face." While Mabel went to wipe off the ketchup, I pitched in and helped Jacy, who'd already begun to clean up the mess, which had, after all, been partly her fault.

Patrea had watched the whole thing play out with an air of fascination. "You're all certifiable, do you know that?"

"See what I said?" I'd forgotten all about Summer until she spoke up again. "Under all that bluff and bluster,

163

Mabel's a really nice person. The patron saint of lost women."

Since I couldn't ask outright, I quirked a brow at Summer.

"Thea's kind of a hard case. I know she comes off as a snarky know-it-all, but she's just dealing with some stuff. You could go easier on her."

I filed the question away under the list of those to ask the next time I had Summer alone. It was a long list and getting longer by the hour.

In the end, Mabel agreed to cater Patrea's wedding without even an ounce of fuss about being her second choice.

"That was easier than I thought it would be," Patrea said when we were back in the car. "And I didn't even need you to run interference."

"Good, then you won't need me to go with you when you set up the menu."

"Nope." Back at the office, she pulled up behind my car. "You were right. Mabel is a pussycat."

Chapter Seventeen

I did my own hair on the second day of the trial. It might not have been salon-perfect, but when I walked into the courtroom, I felt more confident than before.

The judge reminded me I was still under oath, and the dance began. Paul never looked at me, not once, during the entire time his attorney attempted to paint me as an opportunist who only married him for his money.

I felt the jury watching me watch Paul as Peterson used my background, my net worth, and that of my family to paint me as an opportunist. I answered what felt like a hundred questions, and also the same question a hundred times.

"No, I did not marry Paul for his money. I married him because I loved him." My ex-husband finally looked up, and I let my gaze bore into his when I said, "I loved you."

Peterson declared himself done with me, and the prosecution took over. No matter how things turned out, I'd held up. The iron band around my chest fell off.

The rest of my testimony concerned the forged banking statements, which Peterson had patently tried to gloss over as they were the more damning to his case. After what felt like an hour, the judge dismissed me for the final time, and I returned to my seat to watch the rest of the proceedings.

"You were awesome," Patrea whispered and patted my shaking hand. "I think you tipped the jury."

She wasn't wrong. In the face of my unshakable testimony, Peterson lost his edge. Maybe stacking the jury with women hadn't been such a good idea after all. After closing arguments, the judge sent the jury out to deliberate and called a recess.

"Do you want to stay and see what happens?" Patrea asked.

I thought about it for a split second and shook my head. "It doesn't matter to me anymore. If I'm not required to be here, we can go home."

As I turned to do just that, I very nearly plowed into Paul's mother, who'd come up behind me. Her feet hadn't made a sound on the carpet.

"I'm sorry, Tippy," I said. "I didn't see you there." I tried to keep the frost from my tone but didn't succeed as well as I'd have liked.

"Can we talk?" She ignored my apology. "Please, Everly. There's something I'd like to say to you. In private."

Patrea and I exchanged a look, but I left the courtroom with Tippy and followed her down the hallway to an alcove between two columns that flanked a painted portrait of some past judge or other.

"Everly, I'm sorry. I had no idea to what lengths Paul had gone. I never suspected he would do anything like this."

Too little, too late.

"But you had no problem believing whatever he told you when we split. Let me guess, you thought I was a gold-digger, right?"

She had the grace to turn her eyes down. To think I'd once found her grace and demeanor worthy of emulating was another blow to my ego. Worse, I'd compared my mother to her. I was the worst daughter in the history of daughters.

"You have every right to be angry. I see that now, and I wanted you to have this. Consider it an apology or a token of our thanks for everything you did for the foundation."

Tippy pressed an envelope into my hand, gave me one more look. "If it helps, I really do think Paul had genuine feelings for you."

Heat prickled over my face. "Well, you should have taught him not to treat people like dirt. Or else not to think with what's in his pants."

That last crack might have been a bit much because Tippy's mouth dropped open, then closed with a snap. "I am sorry," she said in a remote, wooden tone, then walked away.

After she'd gone, I stuffed the envelope in my purse and took a moment to decide how I felt about what had happened. Bewildered was the best word that came to mind.

"What was that all about?" Patrea asked when I rejoined her.

"Not here. Can we please leave now? I think I've had all the Hastings I can take for one lifetime."

We made it as far as the second hallway turn when I felt another hand on my arm.

"Everly." I heard Paul's voice, shook him off, and kept walking. Maybe it wasn't one of those wind in the hair walks, but it sure felt good to leave him in the dust.

Halfway back to Mooselick River, Patrea's phone rang. She pulled over to answer instead of putting it up on the car's Bluetooth.

"Heard," she said in the clipped tone she used for professional calls.

There was a moment of silence before she thanked her caller and hung up, so it startled me half to death when she let out a whoop.

"The jury came back in record time and with a conviction. He got three years."

Stunned, I slumped in my seat and tried to decide if it was reasonable to feel guilty because I didn't feel guilty over feeling vindicated.

Hey, I never said I wasn't a bag of weird. Feelings are complicated.

"He'll get time served and probably more taken off for good behavior, so I'll be surprised if he does more than six months. And it will be a low-security facility, which I'm betting Peterson gets dialed down to house arrest, but even so, he'll do time. He should have been up for accessory to murder, but for once, his daddy couldn't buy him a free pass."

I think I muttered something, then Patrea said, "You didn't tell me what Madeleine wanted."

"Oh, I forgot. She wanted to apologize. I think for the way she treated me more than the way Paul did. She gave me something." I fished around in my purse and pulled out the envelope.

Patrea had pulled back out onto the road after she'd hung up her phone. Now, she pulled back over. "Open it. I don't even care if it's personal, I'm dying to know, and you'd have told me anyway, so just dispense with the dance of propriety and show me."

She was right on all counts, so I slid my finger under the flap. "She probably named a star for me or something."

Patrea snorted. "You give her too much credit for imagination. It's more likely she donated to the ballet in your name."

But we were both wrong, I saw when I pulled out the check Tippy had written from her private account. There was a handwritten note from her, but I didn't get a chance to read it before Patrea caught a good look at the check.

"Holy crap, that's a lot of zeros. At least she waited until after the trial, so she didn't intend it as a bribe."

"I'm not cashing it, so it doesn't matter what she wants to call it." Slow fire burned in my blood as I crammed the check and unread note back into the envelope and threw it in my purse. "This just goes to show they never knew me at all."

Before pulling back onto the road, Patrea said, "What it shows is the way they judge everyone by their own values. It's human nature, so maybe in this one instance, you could overlook the insult."

"I guess." We were passing the little store I'd stopped at on my way back to town the day my life changed for the better. "Hey, stop here, and I'll buy you lunch."

"Here? Really?" But Patrea pulled in anyway.

"Trust me, it's mostly sandwiches, but they make their own bread, and it's fabulous." Plus, it would be a bookend moment for me. To mark the end of this chapter of my life. Bookend, bookmark…I know they're not the same thing. Cut me a break.

Chapter Eighteen

The day after the trial ended, I learned Patrea had been holding back on things to do with the wedding when a text hit my inbox.

—One of the cousins called to say he'd trained his dog to carry the rings down the aisle.

—Your cousin, or his?

—What difference does it make?

—Just curious.

—His. I'm saying no.

Then another from her.

—What's a polite word for tacky?

I laughed out loud.

"Are you alone?" Drew came in as I was in the middle of unloading the dishwasher. He glanced around the kitchen. We'd decided to allow Summer back so long as she kept herself under tight control. He still hadn't decided if he was ready to meet her in the flesh...or ectoplasm, I suppose.

Secretly, I was happy not to tell her she could show herself to people if she really wanted to. The last thing I needed to do was pave the way for a series of Summer sightings around town. Better to keep the visitations contained to just me if I could manage it. Still, the decision weighed heavy, created one or two uncomfortable moments between us.

"I am. Summer went off in a huff when I decided to order takeout lasagna instead of letting her talk me through making it from scratch. I said I'd had a long day, she said cooking was a good way to release stress, I said I'd rather take a long, hot bath. She got feisty, and then she left."

"Lasagna sounds good, whether from scratch or not."

He'd come up behind me as I put the last glass away, leaned down to nuzzle his face against my neck, his lips roaming gently along the plane of it until they settled into the sensitive spot just below my earlobe. "But you taste better. I could feast on this spot for a week."

I tilted my head to give him better access. "Please, do." The man could stir me up with only a look. When he used his mouth and hands on me, I turned to liquid heat. Somewhere, way in the back of my head, I heard Jacy saying if Drew couldn't accept my ghosts, he wasn't the man for me.

This was the moment where I needed to decide what I wanted from him. He wasn't Paul, and I wasn't the same Everly I'd been even a year ago. That Everly wouldn't have pushed for what she wanted because she hadn't been tested enough to know her limits or her strengths. I didn't want to be her anymore.

As much as I didn't want to, I pulled back from him and tried to get control of my breathing.

"Drew, we need to talk."

"The dreaded phrase no one ever wants to hear." He let me go and tried to make a joke of things. "Is it the wet towels on the bathroom floor?"

"If it was, would you stop putting them there?"

"I'd try. I can't promise I'd remember every time." We settled across from each other at the kitchen table. "But if it's a deal-breaker, I'll give it a shot."

"I'll remember you said that." If things didn't end right here, anyway. "But you know this isn't about your deplorable bathroom habits." I fiddled with my hair, which is something I do when I get nervous. "There's no ghostly equivalent of hanging a tie on the doorknob. They come, and they go whenever they want, and they hardly ever follow the rules."

It was an encouraging sign when he reached for my hands and held them across the table. Maybe the hair fidgeting bothered him, or maybe he wanted to give comfort in an awkward moment because that was the type of man he was—the type with a solid core of unwavering decency that only made me love him more.

"I expect you'll feel like you're living with invisible toddlers half the time," I said matter-of-factly, "and it won't be easy. I'm not used to translating from ghost to living, so if I forget, you'll have to remind me. Also, you should meet my friend Kat. She's the medium who talked me through several freak-outs, and she could answer your questions better than I can."

Jacy wasn't wrong. If Drew couldn't accept my ghosts, he wasn't the man for me, but if I couldn't figure out how to make the process easier for him, then I didn't deserve him anyway.

He still hadn't said anything, but then, I hadn't given him much of a chance. "This is my life. It's full of things that are both weird and wonderful. I'll do everything I can to minimize the weirdness, but If you want me, you'll have to learn to deal with a few things. So, I guess, that's it."

The doorbell signaled, and I went to collect the dinner I wasn't sure I'd be able to eat.

"My turn?" Drew said when I returned. He'd already set the table because he's thoughtful like that.

"Sure."

"Okay, I know this thing between us happened fast, but when you know, you just know. It's the Parker way. We're corny, and we believe in love at first sight. Or at least my parents do. That's how it happened for them."

My stomach settled.

"But—" I began, and he held up a finger to stop me.

"It's still my turn."

"Okay."

"There are a hundred different things about you that I love, and maybe your ghosts aren't on the list, but so what? People aren't made up of pieces and parts you can just swap out for something you like better."

He filled my wineglass with the red he knew I liked, then began to eat as if we weren't in the middle of a potentially relationship-altering conversation.

And maybe we weren't. I have been known to blow things up in my head until they seem much larger than they actually are.

"You have ghosts, and I'd be lying if I said it didn't weird me out a little because I can't see them, too. It's not a deal-breaker for me unless you want it to be. I mean, I'm not sure who knows about the ghosts and who doesn't, and when it's okay to talk about this part of your life. I know I probably shouldn't tell my mother, or she'll bug you to death over every detail. Plus, I have questions."

"So, ask."

He did, and we talked all through dinner, which tasted much better since it wasn't spiced with worry anymore. I told him everything I knew about Summer's case and my suspicions. It helped to talk it all out.

"The husband should be my prime suspect because he mistreated Summer. His girlfriend said he was over there a lot, so he could have put the poison in something she'd eventually use. That's means and opportunity. His name was on the mortgage still, and he didn't waste any time moving back into the house, so that's motive."

"But you don't think he did it. Why?"

I drummed my fingertips on the table while I reasoned it out. "Because he wanted to control her, not kill her." I shrugged. "That's my gut feeling on it, anyway."

Molly padded into the kitchen, sat by the back door, and looked at me expectantly. I opened the door so she could go out, left it open for her return.

"Who's next on the list?"

"Well, Ernie's looking at Mabel, but there's no evidence against her and no motive. Besides, poison wouldn't be her choice of weapon. It's too cold-blooded for someone with her temper."

"What about the new girlfriend?"

"Peggy's on my list, but close to the bottom. She already got the guy—booby prize though he may be—so why get rid of someone who's not even an obstacle?"

Except most of what she'd said about Summer indicated a level of jealousy, so I couldn't give her a pass even if I didn't think she was bright enough to pull off a murder.

"Robin has a theory that Frank Bodine was the real target. But then, Robin's elevator doesn't go the top floor." She'd also mentioned something else that might have been bothering Summer. I made a mental note to track her down and find out what.

Molly wandered back in and settled under the table between our feet.

"This case is a car stalled on the tracks waiting for the train to come along and smash it to smithereens."

"What will happen if you don't find the killer?"

I swallowed the rest of my wine in one gulp. "How do you feel about a Three's Company living arrangement?"

"A what?"

"Sorry, I forget not everyone grew up with a father addicted to old sitcoms. Three's Company, one man living with two women."

"As long as one of them is you." Drew toasted me with his beer bottle.

"Well, I'd rather Summer not become a permanent resident, so I'm hoping the lab comes back with something useful. The only thing I know for sure is the poison wasn't in the angelica extract Summer added to the lemon sorbet. That's not a lot to go on, but enough to take Leandra out of the picture." I grinned. "Do you know, she offered to give everything in the café the sniff test. Said when it came to hemlock, her nose was more reliable than any lab. I recommended Ernie take her up on the offer, but he respectfully declined."

"You could talk to Margo Bodine," Drew suggested.

That might help, but I didn't know her and didn't think she'd be receptive if some stranger knocked on the door and hit her with a bunch of questions. What I needed was an ally or a solid reason for making contact.

If only I knew someone in town who knew everyone and had no qualms about poking her nose in where it didn't belong.

"Drew, you're a genius. Excuse me, won't you?" I rose, retrieved my phone, and called Martha Tipton. The conversation took a minute or ten, but at the end of it, Martha and I had a tentative date to visit Margo the next day.

"There, that's done. In the meantime, I could ask Summer what she served that night. I should have thought of it before, but I have been a little preoccupied with my own drama. I feel bad about not giving her my best, but this would be a good start, and she should be able to tell me that much without being poofed."

Drew paused in the process of putting a forkful of food in his mouth and said, "Being poofed? I don't understand."

Then I had to explain what happened when ghosts tried to talk about their deaths. "I assume it's some cosmic rule, and there's a good reason for it, but it's the kind of thing that makes every investigation more difficult."

"It's like in the Dresden Files," Drew said.

"I don't understand." He'd just talked me into reading the series, but I hadn't cracked the first book yet.

"In the books, the faeries can't lie. Not outright, anyway, so they have to be creative in how they couch things if they want someone to believe an untruth."

I frowned. "I don't get how that helps me with my problem. The ghosts aren't trying to lie to me. They're just prevented from talking about certain things."

"Right." He put his silverware down on his empty plate and leaned back in his chair. "So, this is the flip side of the faerie thing. You need to approach the problem from the side, find the nuanced questions that let them tell you things without invoking the poof rule."

"You have a devious mind, Parker."

"Wasn't me, blame Harry Dresden," he said. "When do you think Summer will show up again?"

"Hard to say. She was pretty ticked off about the lasagna. She takes her cooking seriously, but her way of relieving stress isn't the same as mine."

"I know a better method," Drew said. "We'll take care of the dishes later."

And we did. Much later.

Chapter Nineteen

My inbox listed more texts from Patrea the next morning.

—*Mabel won't tell me what she's putting on the menu.*

—*My mother is coming to visit.*

—*She's bringing my grandmother's wedding broach.*

—*She wants to meet the caterer to discuss her dietary restrictions. How bad do you think Mabel will kill me?*

The fourth was a photo attachment of a perfectly lovely, jeweled broach that wouldn't go with Patrea's dress at all.

"What's in here? Cement blocks?" I asked as I struggled to lift the box Martha told me to carry to the car.

"The church put together a bereavement box for Margo, and since we're going there anyway, I thought we could take it along." She flipped open the top to show me an assortment of canned and boxed goods along with a

Bible and some pamphlets meant to ease the troubled soul.

"Are you sure it's not too early for a visit? What if Margo is a late sleeper?"

"She's awake, and she's expecting us," Martha assured, then amended, "Me. She's expecting me. What with all the division in town, I thought it best to let her know I would be coming by, so I called her first thing this morning."

"Does Margo work?"

"Oh, sure. She's an administrator in the county extension office or maybe a secretary. Something like that. She's on leave until after the funeral."

I didn't point out the difference between administrator and secretary because I wanted to stay on Martha's good side for the moment.

"What is the extension, exactly? I keep hearing about it, but I guess I'm not sure what they do there other than maybe offer some classes for hopeless brown-thumbers like me."

"They do a bit more than that. Weren't you ever in 4-H?"

"Girl Scouts, but I've heard of 4-H. I just thought it was more for farm kids."

Martha bristled. "What is wrong with farm kids?"

Two minutes in a car with Martha brought on the desire to repeatedly slam my hand into my forehead.

"I never said there was. I just thought you had to raise goats or cows to be in 4-H. We didn't own either of those because we lived in town, and so I was a Girl Scout."

If you think a ghost gives off a chill, you should feel the ice coming off Martha when she gets herself into a snit. The car turned positively arctic for a second or two, and then she thawed.

"I suppose that makes sense," she said. "Anyhow, the cooperative extension oversees the 4-H program. I've also called on them to help identify plants, and they were quite helpful with telling me how to get rid of that Japanese knotweed my neighbors planted. It took over my rosebushes and was creeping into my peonies, besides. Nasty stuff, hideous to root out."

Half of her diatribe sounded like gibberish to me.

"So, would it be safe to say Margo knows something about plants?"

"Margo is the president of the horticultural society," Martha said. "How could you not know that?"

"I didn't know there was a horticultural society, so it's a safe bet I wouldn't be able to name the president of it." Getting snippy with Martha never made things easier, so I gentled my tone.

"Do you think, with her special knowledge and all, Margo might have realized she and her husband had ingested poison?" I knew—to stick with the current conversational theme—the best way to plant seeds of curiosity in Martha's head.

"Oh," Martha's hand went up to cover her heart, but her eyes sparkled with interest. "I never thought of that. How awful for her. I do hope she isn't sitting alone and dwelling on the horror of it all. Do you have another appointment this morning?"

"I'm on call, but I don't have anything pressing. Why?"

"Well, I think we should offer to provide Margo a listening ear. Such tales grow less tragic when they're brought out into the light of day, and it might help her feel better if she talks it out."

Bingo.

"If you think we should, then I'm certainly willing." I felt a little slimy for having used such blatant manipulation, but let's be honest, Martha would have pried into Margo's business whether I pushed her into it or not. I'd only bought a tiny bit of insurance to make sure she did it in front of me, that's all.

With Martha's guidance, I pulled up in front of a typical northeastern farmhouse dressed in silver shakes and surrounded by the proverbial picket fence.

I caught the twitch of a curtain falling back into place. Margo must have been watching for us. "Nice place," I said.

"These old homes take a lot of upkeep. This is a lot of house for a woman alone."

"My house is just as big, and I didn't hear you singing that tune when you talked me into buying it."

"I did no such thing." Martha's attempt to pull off an air of insult fell flat. She'd railroaded me, and we both knew it.

But I didn't care. I smiled at her. "I'm not complaining because it turned out well. I couldn't be happier in my new home." Unless someone came up with ghost repellent.

She reached over and patted me on the knee. "Martha knows best, dear."

I let that one go by without comment and considered it my good deed for the day. Or one of them. Carrying the heavy box was another.

Cementing my theory she'd been watching for us, Margo opened the door before we could mount her porch steps, then stood squarely in the opening to block our entrance.

"It was nice of you to come, Martha, but completely unnecessary. As you can see, I'm doing well enough."

Tied around her neck with an intricate knot, the ends trailing, the bold, geometric print of Margo's silk scarf stood out against the unrelieved white of her outfit and made her skin look that much paler. It was a lot of look for this early in the morning.

"I would expect nothing less from a woman with your grace and fortitude," Martha laid it on a bit thick. "I'm so sorry about Frank. Such a tragic loss. Is there anything we can do to help ease your burden?"

"Um, Martha, I'd greatly appreciate it if we could ease *my* burden. This box feels like it's getting heavier by the minute."

"Oh, dear! I almost forgot about you for a minute there. Just carry it right on inside, won't you?"

"I don't—" Margo hesitated, but she couldn't refuse without coming off poorly, so she stepped back and directed me toward her dining room.

"Just put it on the table, and I'll deal with it later."

Having used me to get inside, Martha circled the table, pulled out a chair, and settled in. You can dress up a steamroller in a wool shawl, but getting in its way still won't be a fluffy or pleasant experience.

"Martha, I was just—"

"My dear girl, you're as pale as a ghost. You mustn't try to carry your burden of suffering alone. Tell Martha all about it. You'll feel better."

Margo's eyes narrowed slightly. Martha doesn't do subtle and well-meaning; there could be no mistaking this visit for anything other than a fishing expedition. Somewhere in the house, a clock chimed the half-hour, and as the tone died away, Margo gave in to the inevitable, but not in the way, I think, Martha expected.

"Will it? Will it really make the nightmare go away to describe my husband's final moments to you, Martha Tipton? Will telling you I could have stopped him dying make me feel better? Or that I should have listened to my instincts when Summer stumbled into my house, looking like death warmed over?"

Sometimes, I wonder if I'm a good person. I'd come here to help Summer, but at what cost to Margo? Shoulders hunched, she sat and glared at us with fierce eyes.

"My husband is dead, and I'll have to live with my part in it for the rest of my life. Is that what you wanted to hear? Because talking about it doesn't change anything for me. I hope it makes you feel better. Now, if you don't mind, I'd like to be alone."

On my way out, I laid my hand on Margo's stiff, unyielding shoulder. "I am sorry, Margo. Truly."

Subdued, Martha said nothing and kept saying nothing until I stopped in her driveway to drop her off.

"You really should have respected Margo's privacy. I can't believe I let you talk me into going over there and bothering her like that."

I guess I had that one coming.

Chapter Twenty

After half a morning spent with Martha, I needed comfort food—to be honest, I needed booze and chocolate, but I'm not much of a day drinker, so I opted for a late breakfast at the Blue Moon. I arrived at the beginning of the pre-lunch lull. If not for the rattle of dishes in the kitchen, you'd have thought the place was empty.

"Nope," Mabel barked from the kitchen when she looked up from whatever she was doing and saw me.

"What did I do?" I couldn't remember doing anything that would annoy her to the point she wouldn't serve me. "You can't still be mad about the ketchup."

"I meant," she rolled her eyes and shook her head, "I'm not letting you order off the menu. I've got something I want you to try."

"Okay." I craned my head to see if I could get a look at what smelled so good. "I'm game. What is it?"

"Hold your horses, and you'll see."

"Where's Thea today?"

"Meeting at the school about her kid. She'll be back before the lunch rush."

A minute or two later, Mabel set two plates in front of me, used a white cloth to clean a barely visible drop of something off the rim of one of them. This was not diner food. Or at least not the diner food Mabel usually served.

"Short ribs braised in red wine with roasted seasonal vegetables." She pointed to the first plate. "And this is Chicken Francaise, and haricot verts sautéed with bacon and slivered almonds."

There was not a piece of curly kale anywhere in sight.

"This looks amazing. I didn't know you could cook like this." I used the side of my fork to cut through succulent beef cooked to perfection, took a bite, closed my eyes, and sighed. "It tastes better than it looks. Is this for Patrea's wedding?"

"Of course. You didn't think I'd serve meatloaf and sweet potato pie at a wedding, did you? I'll add a salad and one or two bread options. Because I don't picture Patrea's family as being buffet people, I went with dishes that work well as a family-style meal at each table."

She'd seasoned the roasted vegetables—potatoes, carrots, and parsnips—with both fresh and dried herbs that enhanced the flavors rather than competed with them.

I couldn't wait to dig into the chicken, and I didn't care that Mabel stood with arms crossed over her chest and watched me eat. The food was so good, I wouldn't have cared if I were the prime exhibit in a people aquarium.

"What is in this chicken?"

"It's coated with herbs and breadcrumbs, then topped with a lemon caper sauce."

Eating the chicken was almost a religious experience. "Where did you learn to cook food worthy of a five-star restaurant? And why are you torturing Patrea by not telling her what you're planning to cook?"

After rounding the counter, Mabel sat next to me and answered the last question first.

"Figured she deserved it for making assumptions. I earned a bachelor's from the CIA during my derby days. Got a job at Le Cirque and worked my way up from Commis Chef to Chef de Partie before moving back home to open this place."

So, her roller derby past wasn't just a rumor.

"I had no idea. But why—" I trailed off because I couldn't think of a way to frame the question that wouldn't come off as a disparaging opinion of the diner.

"Customer expectations and simple economics. Mooselick River folk expected your basic diner fare, so that's what I've tried to give them. Comfort food, made from scratch, with a little of my own flair. I don't get to cook like this very often."

"Well, you should. Elevated diner fare is a big thing these days, and if you served these ribs, even as a daily special once a week, I guarantee you'd have a hit on your hands. I haven't even finished them, and I'm already craving more."

It wasn't every day a person could make Mabel blush. I'd only ever heard of it happening once before when Leo Hansen made a spectacle of himself by declaring his love for her in song.

"And, Mabel," I said, "You need to put Patrea out of her misery. Call her in and let her see what you can do. She's got enough going on without needless panic over fantastic food."

"Party pooper," Mabel judged, but I figured she'd do as I asked. "Summer would have done a bang-up job. I feel bad, you know?"

"Since you brought up the subject of Summer, I remember you said something about owing her for some reason, but I didn't get a chance to ask what it was."

As if someone cut the string holding her upright, Mabel's shoulders slumped. She put her elbows on the table and dropped her head in her hands.

"I killed her." It came out muffled, but that's what I thought I heard her say.

"You did what?"

"You heard me. I killed Summer. Or I might as well have."

Shock hit me like a bucket of cold water thrown in my face. "Explain yourself, and it had better be good."

"She used to come by some nights when her husband worked late or early in the morning to help me do prep work. I knew he kept a tight fist, so I'd slip her a few bucks, and we'd talk while we worked. About recipes and cooking mostly. You didn't have to do more than look at her to tell she was lonely."

"Leandra said much the same." What sounded like a fleet of motorcycles cruised past the diner making too much noise for us to speak. When the rumble died away, Mabel picked up her story.

"Anyway, this one morning, I had rhubarb pies going, and Summer asked if I'd ever tried adding angelica to them. She said she had an old recipe book that used to belong to her grandmother, one of those Rebekah cookbooks, and it called for adding a pinch of angelica to the pie to cut the tartness."

It didn't take a crystal ball to see where this was going.

"And it just so happened you knew where it grew wild, so you showed her where to look, and now you feel like her death is somehow your fault."

"That's about the long and short of it," Mabel said.

"Tell her she's an idiot." For once, I didn't jump when Summer popped up on the other side of the counter. If there was a perfect moment for her to show up, this was it.

I'd never hugged Mabel before. Most people wouldn't dare, and if I'd have thought about it for longer than a split second, I might have changed my mind, but the poor woman felt miserable, and I wanted to comfort her.

"I'm sorry you lost your friend."

And then, I sort of broke my rule about messages from beyond the grave. "But you're an idiot if you think you had anything to do with her death. It was tragic, and way too early, and just overall a crying shame, but it was not your fault, and if she were here right now, I know she'd be saying the same thing."

Take that Harry Dresden and your faerie ways of talking around a thing.

Most people also wouldn't dare call Mabel an idiot. At least not to her face. When she didn't put on her roller derby fight face and bash me into a puddle, I figured we'd hit a whole new level in our relationship.

Plus, the diner door opened right about then, and Mabel was too smart to kill me in front of a witness. Of course, when that witness turned out to be Robin Thackery, all bets were off.

"Hey, Robin," Mabel said. "What can I get you?"

"Grilled cheese and a bottle of Coke."

Robin locked eyes with me and crooked her finger, so I joined her at a table in the center of the empty diner. Summer hovered along behind.

"Be careful what you order," Robin whispered. "Get something she can't possibly poison."

My eyebrows shot up so fast, I felt my forehead wrinkle. "Like grilled cheese?"

"Sure. Everyone knows cheese slices come individually wrapped, so it's safe, and she uses store-bought bread."

My left eye wanted to twitch. Even Summer couldn't hold back a grimace over that twisted piece of logic, and when I shot her a look, she shrugged. "I didn't say she was the brightest person I knew, just that she was a good friend, and she means well. In her own way."

To Robin, I said, "Mabel didn't kill Summer. They were friends."

"I know they were friends, but since when has being friends stopped a murderer?"

Because she made a good point, I sighed and changed the subject. It wouldn't benefit either of us to get stuck in a loop of Robin-logic, which was an oxymoron, and one I didn't have time for.

"The other day, you mentioned Summer had something else going on when she passed. Can you tell me what that was? It might help figure out who killed her."

"I know who killed her," Robin flashed a look toward the kitchen.

Knowing I'd regret it, I asked the burning question. "Then why would you eat here?"

"Because I'm hungry, and I only have a half-hour break for lunch, and it's the closest to the store."

Mabel delivered Robin's lunch, and as she did, gave me a wink. Apparently, she'd heard our conversation and wasn't too bothered. When Mabel left, Summer blinked out as well, leaving me alone with Robin.

"The new owners are really nice. They're fixing the place up a lot, and we're going to start selling pizza and sandwiches from the deli."

Mentally, I face-palmed. Physically, I merely sat stunned. "There's been pizza and sandwiches available in the deli the entire time since I moved back to town."

"Oh, I know," Robin said.

There was buzzing in my head.

"What else was bothering Summer? It's important, Robin. I really need to know."

"What?" She looked at me like I'd asked her the square root of pi.

The buzzing went up an octave, and it wasn't only in my head. I checked my phone and found my ringer was somehow set to vibrate, and I had two calls from a tenant.

"You said there was something else besides the divorce. What was the other thing?"

Robin stopped chewing, her face blank while she thought. I could almost hear the hamster wheel whirring.

"Oh, that was nothing, really. Just that Peggy Sullivan called her a couple of weeks ago and said she wished Summer were dead."

Seemed like this was information I should have already had. The urge to reach out and choke Robin was strong, but not as strong as the urge to tell Summer she was on her own.

Chapter Twenty-One

"It was working fine yesterday," said Angie, the harried tenant who'd called me about a badly plugged toilet. "And now it keeps overflowing."

Maybe if you quit flushing it...is what wanted to fly out of my mouth, but I managed to retain a tight smile while I pulled on a pair of heavy rubber gloves. Then, I used an old plastic container to dip out enough water to try the plunger she hadn't bothered to use. I'd already mopped at least three flushes worth of water from the floor and just wanted this to be over soon.

At least the one-piece vinyl had kept the wetness pretty well contained. I wouldn't have to get someone in to repair water damage on the ceiling below. Sometimes it's the small things that are the biggest blessings.

I couldn't be much more than annoyed with the poor woman since she had three kids under the age of five vying for her attention, and none to gently, either. A boy who, on any other day, I'd have called adorable, kept running past the bathroom door yelling at me to hurry up.

"Go use the one downstairs," the tenant—whose name I'd momentarily forgotten because the noise level in the house was off the charts—told him, her tone getting louder with each repetition.

"We'll get you fixed right up. If this doesn't work, I've got a guy who will come over and take a look at it, okay?"

The baby on her hip—a little girl with pink cheeks and a tangle of white-blond curls—stared at me as if I'd come up from the floor in a cloud of brimstone and hellfire. Every time I spoke, she squeaked and buried her head against her mother's neck.

"Can you hand me that...never mind." I grabbed for the plunger and put it to work, but the water level stayed the same.

"You want me to try it now?" Said the tenant as she reached for the handle.

"No!" That time I did shout. "Not yet." I went to work with renewed vigor and was rewarded by the faintest sound of draining water. The level dropped half an inch.

"It's working," I said, and then realized my error when she slammed the handle and overflowed the thing again.

Some days, I hate my job. I know exactly how it sounds when I say that since more than half the time, I get paid for doing nothing, but plunging toilets ranks just below chicken plucking on the list of things I'd rather not do.

"Please, Angie," I begged. "Go ahead downstairs and tend to the kids. I'll take care of this and be right down."

Seeming reluctant to leave me alone, she took some urging before she did as I asked. Grateful, I closed the door behind her and let out a sigh when the noise level reduced from a scream to a hum. Halfway through mopping up the newest puddle, my phone rang.

"Preliminary tox screens confirmed hemlock poisoning, which we pretty much already knew," Ernie Polk didn't bother with such niceties as phone manners. He just got to the point.

"Okay," I said.

"The hemlock was in a container of lemon sorbet," he continued as if I hadn't spoken. "Margo Bodine confirmed her husband ate an entire bowl while she only took a few mouthfuls. She said it tasted off to her, but Frank didn't seem to notice anything funny."

"I expected as much. When I talked to Margo yesterday, she told me about the sorbet tasting off to her."

There was a pause. When Ernie spoke again, he sounded annoyed. "Frank ingested the poison at least two hours before Summer did. His time of death was later, but only because Margo got him to the ER for treatment, which prolonged his life, but only for a matter of hours. Or did you already know that, too?"

"No, I didn't. What do you think? Does that change your view of the case?"

Another pause. "My view of the case no longer matters because come Monday morning, there is no case. The ME plans to issue the final ruling, and it's going to come down as accidental in both cases. Unless something comes to light between now and then, this is over."

"For you, you mean."

"I'm only telling you what I know," Ernie fell back on the tried and true. "What you do with the information is up to you."

"I might have something, but given the source, I need to fish around a bit more to make sure it's valid information. When I do, I'll loop you in."

"You do that." Ernie dropped the official tone from his voice and sounded frustrated. "I've got nothing to go on but my gut feeling here. I know it was murder, but the evidence doesn't line up, and the only person with means and motive is the ex-husband."

"And you don't think he did it."

"Do you?" Ernie countered.

"No," I sighed. "I didn't get the vibe. If he did it, he deserves an Oscar for his innocent act. It's very nearly the perfect crime."

"I think, this time, someone's going to get away with murder." He hung up, leaving me to stand over the clogged toilet in troubled silence.

"Not if I can help it," I vowed, and went to put my phone back in my pocket, stopped when I heard the text tone.

—*Catastrophe*. Patrea had typed.

—What happened now?

—*Delia's assistant sold my hydrangeas out from under us.*

—I have contacts. I'm sure I can track down more.

—*So does Delia. She already made the calls. There's nothing. Statewide.*

—Then we'll find something else.

—*It won't be the same.*

Annoyed with my life, I put the plunger to work again and took out all my frustrations on the clog.

Finally, the toilet burbled, the water level dropped, and I got a look at the problem. Thankful for the protective coating of my yellow gloves, I reached in and dragged a small, stuffed rabbit out of the drain.

Sopping wet and a bit worse for the wear, the toy went into the trash. If Angie wanted to rescue it, that was her business. Mine here was done.

Chapter Twenty-Two

"You owe me." I crossed my arms over my chest, tapped my foot impatiently on the grass, and gave Leandra my best imitation of my mother's sternest look. "And you know it."

Her chin came up. "Not enough to let you dig up my heirloom hydrangeas. My grandmother planted those with her own hands, and I have to take great care with the soil to make sure they don't change color. They have sentimental value to me, and I'm sorry, but I have to say no."

Days before the wedding, the florist called to apologize that her assistant had sold Patrea's potted hydrangeas without checking to see if they were actually for sale. By the time Delia found out what had happened, it was too late. She could offer similar arrangements in delicate pink or blue, but Patrea had her heart set on snowy white, which were, Delia informed me, a bit of a rarity given the PH conditions in most of the local soil.

As soon as Patrea contacted me in a panic, I went into problem-solving mode, calling every single one of my former party planning contacts—not because I didn't take Delia's word, but because I thought my network might be larger than hers. I was wrong. There wasn't a white hydrangea to be had from any florist in a three-state range, which was as far as I could branch out and still get them in time.

But then, I'd remembered Leandra grew white hydrangeas and figured she'd be eager to help since that was her way. I didn't realize the bushes carried such high sentimental value she'd flat-out refuse.

"I'm sorry. Of course, you wouldn't want to dig up your grandmother's hydrangeas." All the fight gone out of me, I slumped down on a convenient garden bench.

"I'm usually better at crisis mode, but Patrea's all keyed up, and some of her stress has bled over onto me."

On top of the wedding preparations, I still had Summer as a part-time roommate. She wasn't any happier about that than I was, but Monday was coming, and Ernie would have to let this one go down in the books as a series of accidental deaths. A day later, and I still hadn't had time to chase down Robin's lead.

The way it was going, I'd have Summer around for the rest of my life.

Leandra took a seat beside me. "I'm sensing there's something else bothering you." She let her eyes go unfocused. "You're just buzzing with tension."

Uh oh. The last time she'd sensed me buzzing with tension, I'd ended up with a ghost problem. If there was something worse she could do to me, I didn't want to know about it.

"I'm okay. Really."

I slid over half a space just in case proximity bred woo-woo cooties. One dose of those was enough to last me a lifetime.

"I'll figure something else out. Maybe you can help with that. Is there another plant in season we could use instead? I need something that's hardy enough to string lights through and has white blossoms." I ran a hand through my already ruffled hair. I hadn't even taken the time to pull it back like I usually did.

Leandra went so quiet I checked to see if she'd gone into one of her famous trances. I didn't think she had, but the way she moved her head from side to side made it seem like she was in the throes of a major decision.

"If I take you somewhere, you have to promise anything you see will stay just between the two of us."

Good grief. If she was going to take me to her secret pot farm, I didn't think I could make that promise. Jacy would kill me if I held out on her, but Patrea needed flowers, so I took a breath and sold my soul.

Maybe soul-selling was a tad dramatic.

"I...uh...I guess. I promise."

Satisfied, Leandra went back inside to put on shoes for the outing. She returned wearing rubber boots and had another pair in her hand.

"Put these on. You'll need them."

"Do I have to?" Where was she taking me that I'd need pink boots with multi-colored polka dots?

Skeptically, she looked down at my flip-flops and then back at my face. "No. But we're not going until you do."

I'd been outmaneuvered by mother logic. It wasn't the first time. I put on the boots, and things went from bad to worse when she went into the barn and came out driving a beat-up ATV. But I'd committed to the venture, and while I wondered if I should actually have myself committed, I went ahead and climbed on behind her.

She gunned the engine and rocketed around the barn heading for a trail I'd never noticed before. For that matter, I hadn't realized Leandra owned a four-wheeler.

"Did Jacy teach you how to drive?" I shouted into the wind, but I don't think Leandra heard me as she zigzagged around tree branches and raced down a narrow track.

Ten minutes later, after negotiating a series of trails, we stopped on the edge of a small boggy swamp.

"You know," I said as I slid to the ground and mud squelched up around my borrowed boots. "You didn't have to worry that I'd lead anyone to your secret…whatever this is…I don't have the first clue where I even am right now."

"We're out behind Mildred Potter's old place." Leandra pointed toward her right, where I could just barely make out the roofline of an old house in the distance.

"Oh, well then, that clears it right up." Excuse me, but I get sarcastic when I've been hauled off into the middle of nowhere by a madwoman with questionable driving skills. But I followed along behind her as she skirted along the edge of the low-lying wetland area.

Her next comment, however, got my attention.

"Don't get too close to those plants," she pointed, but I wasn't sure which ones she meant. "That's hemlock."

"Really? Where? Show me."

"The tall ones with the white flowers. You can tell because the stems have reddish-purple spots. But don't touch them, or you'll likely end up with some nasty contact burns."

"They look so harmless—even a little pretty."

Leandra shrugged. "That's the way of things in nature sometimes. Pretty but deadly. I learned my lesson about hemlock the hard way." She wiggled one foot free of rainbow-hued rubber and turned it to show me a narrow diagonal scar just above her ankle bone.

"I didn't notice anything at the time, but by that evening, it felt like I'd been burned by a hot poker."

"Looks like the mark I had on my neck for three months after a bad curling iron incident." My hand automatically came up to touch the spot where I'd burned myself. "It looked like a hickey for weeks before it finally faded."

Jamming her foot back in her boot, Leandra gave me a sunny smile and offered her wisdom. "I'll probably have this one forever, but our scars mark the path on the road map of experience."

Keeping her advice in mind, I moved in, but not too close. "Looks like those plants that grow along the side of the road on the way to the lake, only these are a lot taller."

"You mean Queen Anne's lace?"

"I guess. I remember picking a bunch of those flowers and putting them in water with food coloring as an experiment on photosynthesis in grade school. Probably a good thing we didn't get hold of a batch of hemlock." A shudder-worthy notion.

Leandra quirked a brow. "I should hope your teacher was smarter than that. Most people around here know the difference. It's not that hard, really. Queen Anne's lace is in the carrot family. It has hairy stems and smells like carrots. Angelica has a flowery scent, and hemlock smells like—"

"I know." I held a hand up to stop her from saying it again and leaned close enough to get a sniff for myself. The wind picked up enough to send the stalks swaying toward me. I was careful not to touch, but she wasn't wrong about the smell. "It's definitely nothing like carrots or angelica."

"You see. That's what I told Ernie. Anyone who knows anything about flora and fauna can tell the difference. Hemlock and angelica don't even look that much alike."

"If you say so. You were right about the smell, so I'll take your word for it."

"Oh, I'll do better than that. Follow me."

I guess I don't have spidey senses, but my ghostly ones tingled when Leandra led me back past the ATV and cut off the trail into the forest bordering the marshy ground. We hiked up a gentle slope, following a path that looked like it was used regularly. Leandra pointed out various plants along the way.

"Remember," she said. "You can't say a word to anyone about anything you see today."

"Girl Scout's honor." I held up my hand to give the sign, then thought better of it. Leandra was up to something that probably went against the Girl Scout's code of ethics. "Or not. Look, if you've got a hidden pot farm out here, I really don't want to know about it."

Whatever reaction I expected, it wasn't a wide-eyed look followed by a bout of laughing and finger-pointing at my expense. I got annoyed.

"I'm sorry." Leandra wiped away a tear brought on by mirth. "But the look on your face. I just can't." The memory set her off again. For once, I didn't find the hilarity infectious.

"Let me know when you're done." I stalked over to sit, stiff-spined, on a fallen log and wait for her to get control of herself.

It took a minute, and her eyes still sparkled with barely contained mirth when she announced she was done and asked for my forgiveness.

"Tell me what's going on here, and I'll think about it."

"Come on."

I followed Leandra to a small clearing where she stopped and pointed dramatically to a scattered patch of short, otherwise nondescript plants with pretty, red berries. If she hadn't drawn my attention to them, I'd have walked right by without noticing.

"There. That's my secret."

"Okay," I drew the word out long, my tone dry as a pack of Ramen noodles.

Leaning toward me as if someone might hear, she whispered. "It's ginseng."

"Okay," I said again at my normal volume.

"I've been growing it."

I still didn't get it. "Let's just assume for a moment that I have no idea what you're talking about."

Leandra sighed. "Ginseng grows wild in the woods here, but you're not supposed to harvest it because it's considered endangered in Maine, and you can't grow it at home for use in distribution without a permit."

"So, you're doing something illegal."

"Technically."

My brain finally connected a few dots.

"Did Summer know about your ginseng stash?" Her name barely passed my lips before I felt the chill of her at my back.

"Of course." Both woman and ghost said at the same time.

More dots lined up in my head. "And her angelica patch is somewhere nearby?"

"That's where we're headed right now, but I thought I'd take a look at my crop since we're out here and all."

Leandra got down on her hands and knees in the dirt and gestured for me to do the same. I squatted instead.

"You can tell the age of the plant by the number of leaves. This one has four sets of leaflets. That means this one is at least three years old and is technically ready to harvest."

Frowning, I stroked a leaf with my finger. "What's it good for?"

"It's an antioxidant," Summer said.

"Boosts memory, lowers blood sugar, and is a mood enhancer for a start." Leandra supplied. "I use it in several of my tincture recipes."

"But it's illegal?"

"It's not like I'm dealing heroin, Everly." Leandra rarely offered the sharp side of her tongue, but today, I guess I'd earned it. "I'm merely nature's steward. There was only one plant here when I stumbled on this spot. I've taken excellent care to increase Mother Earth's bounty, and I've helped a few people be healthier besides. In the great mother's eyes, I've done nothing wrong."

Arguing with zealots is an exercise in futility. I know; I've been there and done that before. With this particular zealot, in fact. Arguing with Leandra was like trying to stop the tide with a teaspoon.

"This is why you didn't want to show Ernie where Summer got her angelica." Made a lot more sense now.

"Why else?" Summer had drifted off somewhere, but Leandra seemed puzzled by my observation.

"You realize Ernie thought you were covering up for Summer having mistaken the hemlock for angelica, right?"

It felt safe to speak for Ernie since I'd known better, and it still had looked that way to me. He must have been thinking the same thing.

My knees felt like a pair of rusty hinges when I finally couldn't take another second of squatting. Then, I had to give Leandra a hand up. Once on her feet, she didn't let go of my hand.

"You'll keep my secret?"

"Do the people who buy them know what's in the tinctures?"

"Of course. It's not illegal to use ginseng in any preparation. Only to harvest it in the wild with the intent to sell or distribute, or to cultivate it for the same reasons without the proper paperwork. I don't fudge the truth about the ingredients I use, only about where I obtained some of them."

"I won't tell. But you need to look into making it legal to grow at home."

That got a grin out of her. "I plan to do just that now they've legalized the other thing I'm growing at home that you didn't want me to talk about."

Gah.

"Do you still want to see the angelica?"

"Might as well." It didn't look like I could learn anything to help Summer, but I was curious to see the plant anyway, so I followed her to the dappled shade at the edge of a larger clearing. Summer had headed in this general direction but was nowhere in sight.

"You're right." I inspected the angelica, compared it with my memory of the hemlock. "They're not that similar up close, and the difference between the scents is hard to miss. Is this the only place it grows?" Because even considering the ginseng detour, we'd walked far enough from the hemlock for proximity to no longer be a viable explanation for any possible mistake.

"Only place I know of, and Summer would have told me if she'd found more."

Just to make sure Mabel's story checked out, I asked, "Did you find this spot, or did she?"

"She did."

"Do you think her husband killed her?" Leandra knew the situation better than most. Maybe Summer had said something to her that would help me.

She stopped, turned to me. "It would be easier if I did, wouldn't it?"

I'd seen Leandra lose her cool over the years. She was the blow up and clear the air type, just like her daughter—a nice, hot blast of temper, followed by calm and forgiveness. The woman standing before me now was in full possession of her cool, but there wasn't a single sign of forgiveness in her expression. If you'd have asked me before, I'd have said Leandra didn't have this much ice in her. I'd have been wrong.

"Because then, I'd know exactly what to do about him."

I probably should have asked what she meant, but I didn't. If ever there was a time when ignorance was bliss, this was it.

By the time we got back to the ATV, the old Leandra had replaced the scary new one.

"This way," she said and led the way up the gentle slope in a different direction. The ground squelched less under my feet, and the distant house seemed closer as we went. I figured we'd moved onto the property proper when Leandra turned and said, "Mind your step," then pointed to a broken-down section of barbed-wire fence.

We turned right and followed the fence. After years of neglect, the forest had begun to reclaim Mildred Potter's property, but I could tell she'd had a nice lawn back in the day. Now, it looked wild and untamed, as if the perennial flowers had escaped their beds and were at war with the encroaching forest.

"Are we trespassing?"

"Technically, I guess," Leandra admitted. "But I knew Mildred before she passed, and I don't think she'd mind. She was a jolly sort of woman even after she lost her husband. They were never blessed with children, so I have no idea who owns the property now, but no one has been out here for years except me."

She pointed to some bushes almost as tall as me. "In another few days, I'll come back for the blackberries— best in town. I used to come out here with my grandmother to pick them every summer after Milly got too old for it. We'd take her up a few quarts for eating— more on the years she wanted to make jam—and bring home plenty for ourselves. I like to think she's up there, smiling down on me, happy I'm carrying on the legacy."

Only Momma Wade could turn a bout of trespassing into a tribute to the dead.

A veritable thicket of rosebushes barred entrance to the front of the house, reminding me of the thorny vines in the story of Sleeping Beauty, only less sinister. This late in the season, only the red hips and a few stray petals were left to show me they'd have been a lovely mix of pinks, white, and yellow.

"Ta-da," Leandra waved a hand dramatically. At what, I couldn't tell, so I gave her a quizzical look. "Over there," she pointed.

Wedged into the corner almost behind a section of the rose bushes, I caught a flutter of white.

"Millie wouldn't mind a bit if you took a few of her hydrangeas. They're not doing anyone any good out here."

Had I really stooped so low as to steal flowers from a dead woman's yard? What would Patrea think?

At least she'd defend me for free if I got caught.

"You know, my mother used to warn me about falling in with a bad crowd. I don't think she expected it would be the parents I'd have to worry about."

Leandra knew she had me hooked. "I have some burlap sacks and a folding shovel in the saddlebags of the

ATV. Won't take long to dig up what we need, and no one will ever know but us."

"Don't tell me this isn't insurance to make sure I'll keep your little gardening secret." But I followed her down to get the supplies and only barely avoided disaster when I tripped over the downed fence on the way back up.

Flailing, I dropped the burlap sacks and made a grab for the standing part of the fence. Just missing being impaled on a wicked set of rusty barbs by an inch or so, my hand closed over the fluttering cloth I'd noticed earlier. The shred of thin material tore under the force, but I managed to stop my fall.

"That was close." I tucked the remnant into my pocket because I don't like to litter, picked up the sacks I'd dropped, and went off to commit a crime.

Chapter Twenty-Three

The day before the wedding brought several fires to put out and a flurry of texts from Patrea.

—*The rental company brought two extra-long tables, and we're short three of the round ones.*

—Tell them to set the extra-long ones up in a U-shape off the main table. We'll put the immediate family at those, then cluster the round tables in the middle.

—*That's perfect. You rock.*

Then:

—*You took the dresses out of the bags, right?*

—I did. They're hanging in the bedroom upstairs, and they look perfect. Will you please stop worrying?

—*The flowers.*

—Will be delivered to the farm first thing in the morning. Delia has the plans we drew up, and she's on top of it. And before you ask, the stylist called to confirm, she and her team will be here in plenty of time to make us all look pretty.

And finally:

—Drama

—What now?

—One of the uncles just blew into town with a younger woman as his plus-one.

—Yours or his?

—His and the aunt had a meltdown. The uncle wasn't even invited.

At least that one wasn't something I felt the need to fix. Nor was the next one.

—More drama. Pregnant cousin dropped out of college to follow her boyfriend to LA, where he has an audition for a deodorant commercial.

—Yours or his?

—Mine.

"Weddings don't always bring out the best in families," Summer said after reading over my shoulder. "But I wish I'd had cousins at mine."

I set my phone aside, opened the dryer, and began to shake out my colored clothes before folding them.

"Don't I know it," I said. "My folks weren't thrilled with my choice of husband, but the wedding itself went off well enough. What was yours like?"

Summer hovered, cross-legged over the dryer where I usually stacked my folded clothes, so I used the top of the washer instead.

"You know. The wedding went fine. It was the rest of the marriage that didn't work out so well. My mother still isn't—or wasn't speaking to me. She still thinks I was a fool to let Jack go."

Score one for Leandra.

"I'm sorry. I can't say my relationship with my mother went quite so far as yours, but we had some rocky times for exactly the opposite reason. She saw the flaws in Paul long before he showed them to me. What about your dad?"

"Never really had one. My mom raised me alone, so it was always just the two of us—until it wasn't," was all Summer would say on the subject.

"Do you think you could move? I need to get to the dryer vent, and I don't want to reach through you to do it." Touching ghosts feels creepy and also seemed rude under the circumstances.

She obliged, so I pulled out the screen to reveal thick layers of lint.

"You'd save on drying time if you cleared the trap between each load," Summer lectured.

I rolled my eyes and put on my best teenager voice. "Yes, Mom. I know how to do laundry."

The lint made a crackling, paper sound when I peeled it back from the screen.

"And clean your pockets."

As soon as I saw the first tattered shred of water-damaged paper, I remembered putting a folded sticky note in my pocket, but the bit of cloth also embedded in the lint didn't ring any memory bells.

"That looks like silk." Summer didn't actually breathe, but she felt like a cold breath on my neck. I shuddered. "You didn't wash a silk scarf, did you?"

"No, I don't even own a silk scarf." Technically untrue. Catherine Willowby had owned more than a few, and since her stuff was now my stuff...

"Well, that one looks like someone put it through a meat grinder."

I tossed the cloth into the trash along with the lint. "Probably just some trash I picked up somewhere along the line and stuck in my pocket."

My to-do list wasn't getting any shorter while I debated proper laundry etiquette with a know-it-all ghost.

"Hey, any chance you pushed someone to homicidal limits with your constant need to suggest better ways of doing things?"

The question might have been out of line, but it got her out of the laundry room. I had to refold the clothes she flipped in the air on her way out—not a bad trade-off for some peace and quiet. I called Jacy to finalize the plans for Patrea's bachelorette party.

"Everything's set on my end," I said. "I've heard back from all but one person on the guest list, and when I spoke to Miranda, she said she'd locked in the entertainment. I'm dubious because the deposit wasn't that much, but she said to trust her and that this wasn't the first hen party they've thrown at the bar."

"I resent being called a hen," Jacy said. "It's not dignified. I do not cluck."

"We already had dignified at the bridal shower, and also, I distinctly remember some clucking over that Meissen gravy boat," I said.

"Better clucking than pearl-clutching, I suppose."

There'd been some of that as well.

"I've got a customer," Jacy said. "Gotta go. We'll meet you after work to put up the decorations. I'll call if we're going to be late."

"Okay, bye." It was already too late. She'd hung up in my ear.

With all the wedding preparations taking up my time, talking to Peggy Sullivan kept sliding lower and lower on my to-do list. Now, I had the perfect excuse, so I called the salon to see if she had room in her schedule to do another one of her sexy blowouts for me.

"I'm sorry, Peggy called out today. Some sort of personal emergency. I could fit you in if you want." I recognized the dulcet tones of Cindy, the hairdresser who thought Jack was a killer.

"I hope everything works out okay with her, and I appreciate the offer, but it's okay. I'll call back another time."

I still thought my hair looked good when we walked into Cappy's that evening, but *this* evening was all about Patrea, and she looked radiant if embarrassed wearing a plastic tiara with BRIDE in rhinestones across the top.

The first round of champagne—and cider for Jacy— in hand, we took Patrea on a memory walk of the place, pointing out where we'd been sitting the first time she'd laid eyes on Chris, and ending on the dance floor.

"And this is the very spot where you did the sexy dance of love," Jacy said.

Face red, Patrea said, "Are you sure they didn't spike that cider? You're clearly drunk."

"Drunk with love." Jacy teased.

Patrea shook her head, but she couldn't hold back a smile, and then, her face turned serious for a moment. "I'm just going to say this once because I don't do mushy, but I liked the life I had before I came to this place and fell under the small-town spell. I liked my life because it was orderly and easy, all black and white. I never had to worry about coloring outside the lines."

She paused and let her gaze touch each one of us, linger, then move on. "But then there was you—all of you, and Chris, and a whole new world that opened up to me. It's messy and colorful, and I love it. I love you. And I love Chris. And I'm getting married tomorrow."

"Yes, you are. But that is tomorrow. Tonight is your last night as a single woman, so we're going to party up a storm...or is it party down?" Neena tilted her head toward the decorated table.

"I'm not getting drunk," Patrea warned. "I want to be clear-headed and present tomorrow."

"She's only saying that," I said, "because she's afraid her cousin will take advantage of her in a weakened moment and talk her into letting his dog be the ring bearer."

Patrea grinned. "That will not be an issue because I couldn't actually find a polite word for tacky, and now he's not speaking to me. I'm not sure he'll be attending the wedding, after all."

"Sounds like a small blessing to me," Jacy said and linked arms with Patrea. "And I think it's sweet you don't want to be hungover for your big day, but that doesn't mean we can't have a good time."

That good time began with appetizers and a round of drinks once the rest of the guests arrived.

"What do you think the men are up to tonight? Did Chris tell you?" I asked. "Drew wouldn't say a word other than they had big plans."

"No, but I assume he and David cooked something up. Chris has been helping him with some project or other at the inn for the past couple of weeks."

"Really?" I drew the word out long. "Drew, too."

"And Brian," Jacy said.

Any further speculation on the matter ended with the arrival of the food and more drinks. Patrea's cousin partook or more drink than food and regaled us with several childhood stories as she did.

"That's not exactly how it happened," Patrea protested when accused of pilfering a bottle of expensive scotch from her grandmother's liquor cabinet. "I was merely the pawn. Justin was the brains behind the scheme. He knew I'd cry if I got caught, and Mimmie couldn't stand to see me cry, so she'd let me off the hook."

"But you didn't get caught, and Justin drank himself sick. If I remember it right, he tossed his cookies in the downstairs closet and ruined a pair of Ferragamo loafers."

Patrea smiled at the memory. "Wasn't it you who set Mimmie's gazebo on fire, though?"

Taylor made a face. "Don't be dramatic, Treenie. The gardener put it out almost before it started, and Grandpapa wasn't even mad about it."

Treenie? That would come up again.

Patrea caught my amused expression and gave me a mock glare to warn me it had better not.

"Not about the gazebo, but he was none too happy that the gardener used the hose on his last pack of Gauloises."

Neena frowned. "His what?"

"Fancy French cigarettes. Nasty things, too. I remember—" Patrea broke off and stared at something behind me. I turned to look.

Peggy Sullivan hadn't been invited to the party but was dressed to fit in with the theme as she careened toward us like a pinball bouncing off chairs and leaving a line of perplexed patrons—mostly women because of what would come later—in her wake. A crowded drinking establishment is no place to wear the fluffiest wedding dress on the planet, and I wish I could say Peggy made it work, but she didn't.

She finally fetched up at our table when she walked smack into the back of Neena's chair.

"Sorry, sir." Peggy slurred her words, then leaned back to bring Neena's face into focus. She would have fallen if Jacy hadn't reached out to steady her.

"Whoopsie. You're not a sir."

"No," the corner of Patrea's mouth twitched. "She's not. Are you here with someone?"

Where was Jack? I checked the bar as best I could from where we sat and didn't see him anywhere.

The question drew Peggy's attention to Patrea and resulted in a drunken raspberry that sent droplets of spit into Neena's hair. Chairs scraped on the floor as people moved out of the way so Peggy could circle around the table.

A busy bar never goes quiet, but in our general area, the noise level dipped low as people watched the show.

"Ooh! You've got a tiara. I wanted a tiara." She tried to pat Patrea on the head, or maybe to steal the tiara, but missed by about a foot. "You'll make a pretty bride. Hey, do you need a dress? You can have mine."

Reaching back for the zipper, and missing, Peggy spun around three times before she forgot she'd been trying to take off her dress.

"Not as pretty as you."

Throwing her head back, Peggy laughed. "Not anymore." She waggled her fingers to show the lack of a ring, then became engrossed by the motion. As she did, I noted she still had the narrow burn mark on her arm I'd seen the day of the trial. "Called the whole thing off."

Amid the low hum of whispered comments and snickering laughter, Jacy took pity on Peggy.

"Why don't you sit with us, and we'll see if we can't find you some coffee, okay?" Being Jacy, she showed the drunk woman gentle kindness but managed to meet every stare with a fierce glare that encouraged the rest of the patrons to go back to minding their business.

Peggy wasn't having it. "I'm fine. Don't you worry about me." She pulled away and marched back the way she'd come singing a rather flat rendition of Here Comes the Bride. With relief, I saw fellow hairdresser, Cindy, exit the bathroom, notice the empty seat where Peggy should have been, and scan the room for her.

The last we saw of Peggy was poor Cindy wrestling her and her dress out the door.

"Well," I let my tone go dry. "Let's hope Peggy's performance doesn't upstage the actual entertainment."

"Looks like we're about to find out," Neena said as the house lights went dim.

A collective cheer went up when spotlights behind the stage silhouetted five unmistakably male shapes. Another, louder cheer went up when a rock song with a driving beat blasted through large speakers on either side of the stage.

Still in silhouette, the men began to dance, and the women screamed again.

More spotlights flicked on, aimed at the stage, then panning toward the dancers, lighting just their feet before moving upward in a slow tease that revealed them by inches while keeping their faces still in shadow. Up over calves, knees, and thighs clad in muscle-skimming denim, the light paused for a few beats where denim gave way to oiled skin and didn't move again until the cheering went up a notch.

Slower yet, the spots played over rippling muscles.

I don't know if Patrea was the first to realize what was happening, but she was the first on her feet. I didn't catch on until Jacy's elbow slammed into my ribs, and she all but screamed into my ear.

"Those are our men on that stage."

"What?"

Not two seconds later, the spotlight proved her right. Drew, Brian, and David danced beside Chris and his best man, a friend from his time on Broadway. Now, we knew what they'd been doing when they were supposed to be working on the inn. Chris must have been teaching the others some moves because none of the other three had ever danced like that before.

Three seconds later, I decided I didn't mind the deception and settled in to watch the show.

Chapter Twenty-Four

An overnight change in temperatures brought fog and a momentary panic to the morning of Patrea's wedding.

"This will burn off, right?" Patrea repeated as she looked out my front window for the third time. "I don't want to get married on the set of a horror movie."

"It already is, and the weather report says we'll have a sunny day, so stop fretting and eat something before everyone gets here."

Wrinkling her nose at me, Patrea said, "I'm the bride. I should get to decide if I want to eat or not." But she followed me back to the kitchen and settled in with her breakfast.

"Are you nervous?"

"I thought I would be, you know?" She gave Molly a piece of toast crust and then shot me a defiant look when I scowled at her for it. "But this feels too right to be scary even though my life has gone upside down. Chris is my balance."

Then she grinned. "He's the whole package."

"Do not mention the word package after last night."
I shuddered. "I may never get over the experience of
hearing Barbara Dexter discussing which man had the
best package in the ladies' room last night."

Over the next few hours, my house filled with
women, laughter, and the scent of hairspray. Eliza, the
wedding photographer, flitted around with her camera
getting shot after shot of the preparations without being
in the way. Taylor, of course, was the last one to arrive—
and considering the size of the bags under her eyes, the
one most in need of cosmetic enhancement.

"You look fab, Treenie. Vintage suits you," she
offered air kisses. "Point me in the direction of the
bubbly, would you? I could use a little hair of the dog."

"Ten bucks says she's the one dancing on a table
topless by the end of the night," Jacy said for my ears
only.

"Sucker bet." But I made a note to keep an eye on
Taylor during the reception.

Delia sent me photos of the tables with her beautiful
centerpieces against the white linens. When I checked in
with Mabel about the food, she told me to buzz off and
hung up—I assumed that meant she had it under control.

Hours of wedding preparations passed in a haze of
hair and makeup. Shortly after noon, Mabel surprised us
all by sending Thea over with enough sandwiches to feed
an army, but not as much as Thea surprised us by being

pleasant—and that was before Patrea's mother slipped her a crisp hundred-dollar bill for a tip.

As the bride, Patrea set the tone, and the rest of us followed. Since she seemed relaxed and happy, the time passed in similar fashion. The only moment of friction came when Patrea's mother nipped the champagne bottle from Taylor's hand before she could pour the third refill.

"Pace yourself," she said, "until after the ceremony." The iron in her voice left no room for argument. Taylor offered none but stayed at a distance from her aunt, even sitting as far from her as she could during the limo ride to the farm.

Inside the tent set aside for the bridal party's final preparations, Mrs. Heard nearly ruined everyone's makeup when she took Patrea's face between her hands and kissed her daughter on the forehead and then on both cheeks. "Be happy."

"Oh, I will." Patrea pulled her mother in for a hug, then turned to her father and placed her hand on his waiting arm. If he had anything he wanted to say to her, it would have to wait because the swelling strains of the music said it was time.

Lit as much by her own inner glow as by the slanting pink of the setting sun, Patrea pledged her life to Chris as solemnly as he pledged his to her. It was a moment so pure it almost hurt to watch when they took their first kiss as man and wife.

Amid applause, the pastor introduced the newly married couple, and then it was time to follow them back up the aisle. On the way, I noticed some surprises among the faces. Given recent events, I hadn't expected Margo Bodine to attend, but she sat on the groom's side of the aisle, as did Ernie Polk, while Peggy Sullivan had a seat on the bride's.

When we both got a minute, I'd have to ask Patrea how that had happened.

"My wedding wasn't like that." Blatantly ignoring the rules, Summer paced the aisle alongside me. I didn't answer but turned my head and gave her a look. She ignored that, too. "This one will last."

Since I believed the same, I nodded slightly and turned away. When I looked back, she was gone. Good, I didn't need a ghostly distraction in the middle of my Maid of Honor duties.

Those duties kept me busy through the wedding supper, ending with Brian's Best Man toast, right before the cutting of the cake.

"If you haven't seen the groom's cake, you should go look now before they cut it," Jacy said as soon as Patrea and Chris left the table to make their rounds visiting all the tables. "It's freaking awesome. You have to get me the name of the bakery because I totally want something like that for Wade's first birthday."

In the shape of a standing Christmas tree complete with gifts beneath, the cake didn't disappoint.

"Isn't that the cutest thing?" Peggy Sullivan asked as I admired the artistry. "I wonder if the same person did both cakes because the wedding cake is a bit...simple. Or maybe plain is a better word."

No need to ask what Peggy's would have looked like. She'd have gone for something flashy.

"I'm sorry things didn't work out between you and Jack. Do you mind telling me what happened between the two of you?"

The way I figured it, Peggy and Jack were the only two people with a motive for Summer's murder. If Peggy had killed out of jealousy, would she then go and dump the man she'd killed to have? Didn't seem likely to me.

Unless she figured out Jack was the killer—but then, why would she cover for him?

No, whatever Peggy said right now would tell me what I needed to know.

Probably.

Did I mention this case hadn't gone well from the beginning?

"Remember how I told you Jack moved back into Summer's house?"

"Sure."

"He never packed up her things." She shook her head as if still unable to believe the truth. "He said it was a matter of practicality, but her underwear was still in the drawer. What was I supposed to do? I think he wanted me to be her, and that's when I told him it was over."

Probably not Peggy, then. Maybe the burn marks on her arm really did come from a curling iron.

Someone jostled my back in their haste to get to the groom's cake, so I looked for someplace a bit more private and pulled her toward an out-of-the-way corner.

"I have to ask. Did Jack ever threaten you? Or say anything to make you think he might have wanted to hurt Summer? It's important."

Taking the question seriously, Peggy gave it few moments of thought. "Never, and I don't think he'd hurt anyone. I'm just glad I never gave notice on my place. Now, if you don't mind, I've got my sights set on one of the groomsmen."

"Really? Which one?"

She pointed toward David. "The dark-haired one with the brooding eyes. I asked around, and he's single. I'm single. Might as well mingle."

I probably should have warned David, but I didn't. He was a big boy. He'd have to take care of himself. If this were any other time and place, I'd have wanted popcorn while I watched the show.

Hello, square one. Nice to see you again.

"No luck?" Summer's icy presence shivered along my skin.

"I don't think it was Peggy, but that only leaves Jack." I put my hand over my mouth because I didn't want people thinking, *there's Everly Dupree, standing in the corner talking to herself.* Not that *there's Everly Dupree standing in the corner with her hand on her mouth* was a vast improvement.

"Jack wouldn't kill. He had some archaic notions of what a marriage should look like, but if he wanted to kill me, he would have done it before paying for a divorce, not after."

"You should know that on Monday, the ME intends to rule your death an accident. That means we have until then to figure this out. So I need you to help me out as much as you can. Ernie said the poison was in the lemon sorbet, which you brought from home. That means your killer had to have access to your home freezer. Does anyone else have a key to the place?"

Summer shook her head. "No, and now that you mention it, that lets Jack out as well. I added deadbolts after he moved out. A woman living alone can't be too careful. I'm sure you feel the same, but Jack couldn't have gone into the house when I wasn't home. He didn't have the keys."

"Erg," I growled. "I saw you eat that sorbet, so…wait. I saw you eat that sorbet." A drop of oil fell on the rusty wheels of my brain. "I saw you taste it while we were in the café, but the autopsy results put Frank as the first to ingest the poison."

"Does that help?"

"It does. I need to think this through, but not now. This is Patrea's night, and I'm needed." So saying, I left Summer standing alone and returned to the party.

"Where'd you go?" Patrea caught me as I passed by

"I got cornered by Peggy Sullivan while I was admiring the groom's cake. Now that Jack's out of the picture, she's planning to make a play for David."

"She's out of luck," Patrea nodded toward where Neena and David sat in earnest conversation. "I think he's already spoken for."

"They look good together," I said, then spun around when a commotion on the other side of the tent drew our attention. Jacy would have almost won her sucker bet.

"I'd probably better put a stop to that before my mother goes apoplectic."

"No, this is your night. I'll take care of it." Leaving Patrea, I made my way toward where Taylor now danced in front of the band. She wasn't topless yet, but only because she couldn't figure out how to work the zipper of her dress.

"Come on, Taylor." I stepped up to lock her arm against my side and attempt to pull her down from her perch. "You can't be up here while the band is playing."

She resisted, and I redoubled my efforts. So did she.

Across the tent, Drew noticed the scuffle and began to work his way over to help, but I caught his eye, shook my head, and applied the lessons he'd been teaching me for months in self-defense class. I used Taylor's weight against her and had her down before he reached my side.

The only problem was I let go of her too quickly, and she stumbled right into Margo Bodine, who went flying into one of the potted fir trees we'd set up to keep people away from the sound system. I shoved Taylor toward Drew, made a grab for Margo, and pulled her to safety. Or almost anyway, the trailing end of her signature scarf got caught up in the branches and tore, leaving several inches behind.

"I'm so sorry, Margo. I didn't see you there. Are you all right?" I checked her for signs of injury.

"I'm fine." When she saw who I was, she gave me a dirty looked, turned her ramrod-straight back on me, and walked away.

"Well, exchoose you," Taylor slurred, but I barely heard her.

All I could do was stare at the shred of silk while all the clues to Summer's murder clicked into place.

"I hate to do this to you but keep an eye on Taylor. I need to find Ernie Polk."

Chapter Twenty-Five

I dragged Jacy away in the middle of the Chicken Dance.

"What is wrong with you," she batted my hand off her arm. "I'm dancing here."

"Have you seen Ernie anywhere in the past few minutes? It's important."

The gravity in my expression got through to her, but she didn't appreciate my interrupting her favorite wedding tradition. "A bunch of people went outside when the band fired up. He's probably out there, too. Why?"

"I need to find him, that's all." It was too loud to explain why, but Jacy didn't care about the reason, only that I needed help.

"Okay, let's go."

"Act casual," I whisper-warned as we stepped out into the cool, night air. "We're about to catch a killer."

"I love it when we do that." She split off toward the left, leaving me to go right.

That's my Jacy—a pink mini-van driving adrenaline junkie who always has my back. At least this time, I was reasonably sure I wasn't putting her in danger.

Zig-zagging from one cluster of guests to the next, I spotted Ernie, beer in hand, looking out of place in a suit instead of his uniform, talking to Tim from the hardware store.

"Excuse me, Tim." I walked up and looped my arm through Ernie's. He flinched at the unexpected contact. "I need a moment with Ernie, do you mind?"

Coming from the other direction, Jacy joined us as I looked for a quiet spot where no one could overhear.

"It was Margo Bodine." And didn't it just burn my backside that Robin had called it from the start. "She put the poison in the sorbet and fed it to Frank."

"Have you lost your mind? She got sick, too."

I hadn't factored that into my epiphany, but when I did, it still fit.

"Sure, she had to make it look good, right? So she took just a tiny amount. Barely any. Just enough to get sick, too. Then she took the sorbet back to the café. I bet Summer mentioned she'd be there cooking for Patrea's tasting the next day."

It all played out in my head. Margo knocking on the kitchen door, telling Summer there was something funky with the sorbet. I saw Summer picking up a spoon, taking a bite. It did taste a little off, so she took another and sealed her fate.

Just as I saw it, I described the chain of events for Ernie and felt the chill when Summer faded into view.

"That's exactly how it happened." Released from her enforced silence now that the truth was out, she could confirm my theory. "The angelica covered up the scent of the hemlock, and I didn't realize what had happened until it was too late. I just thought I'd come down with the flu or something, and I kept cooking because I didn't want to miss another appointment."

"Doesn't matter," Ernie insisted. "I can't arrest her without proof."

"I have proof...or sort of. Probably not enough, though. Margo left a piece of one of her silk scarves on a barbed wire fence near where she harvested the hemlock."

Ernie shook his head. "Not enough. I need more than circumstantial evidence."

"What if she confessed?" Jacy wanted to know.

"Why would she be stupid enough to do that?" Ernie huffed out a breath. "She's in the clear. All she has to do is keep her mouth shut."

One thing about Jacy, she has a huge heart, and a forgiving one. "I almost feel sorry for her. She'll get away with it, but she'll be haunted by guilt. Isn't that enough?"

Haunted by guilt.

I disagreed with Jacy's point of view, but it gave me an idea.

"Don't ask me why, but I have a feeling she'll talk to me if I can get her alone." Not really alone, but Ernie didn't need to know that. "Ernie, you wait here and stay out of sight. Jacy, you find Margo and say whatever you need to to get her here. I've got something I have to do, it shouldn't take more than a couple of minutes, and I'll be watching for you."

Ernie wanted to refuse, but I reminded him he'd asked for my help.

"I merely kept you informed."

"Yeah, yeah. I know the drill. What I did with the information was up to me. Just trust me, okay? Stay behind the that tree, and don't come out until you've heard what you need to hear."

And not seen anything I don't want you to see.

Reluctantly, he stepped back behind a potted fir while Jacy went to find Margo, and Summer followed me some distance away to where what I had to say wouldn't be overheard.

"How would you like to help me catch your killer?"

"What can I do? I'm a ghost, remember?"

"And what do ghosts do?" She gave me a blank face. "They haunt the living."

Same face.

"Do you remember when you got mad and turned on the stove? Your emotions can have an effect on the living world if they're strong enough."

"So? I don't think shaking the bushes will be enough to rattle Margo's nerves and make her confess."

"No, but you could use that energy to show yourself to her. I think that would do it, but I'm not entirely sure how it works."

Blank face turned to fierce face. "Get her here. I'll figure it out."

It took a few minutes, but that's what Jacy did.

"What's this all about?" Margo said when she saw me waiting alone. "I was just leaving. I probably shouldn't have come. It's too soon."

"Too soon after what, exactly? I know you're not talking about losing your husband."

Could I be any lamer? My stalling technique needed work.

Margo puffed up. "What a perfectly horrid thing to say to me after what I've been through."

Anytime now, I thought hard at Summer.

"Oh, please! You know you—" I felt the prickling on the back of my neck, then saw Margo's face go white. Jacy's too, and wouldn't you know, Drew had seen Jacy trolling the tent and followed her out. He stopped and stared.

"Margo Bodine, you poisoned me, and you must pay." Summer made her voice all deep and scary. "Confess your sins."

A tad dramatic, but hey, whatever it takes.

"No." Margo pointed a shaking finger. "This can't be happening."

"Yes, it can." Summer floated closer. Margo reared back, then gave in to her instincts and turned to run. Except Drew was there, and she slammed right into him. It would have been a fine moment for him if he'd actually been trying to stop her instead of staring at Summer.

"You can run, but you can't hide. Confess, or you will never be free of me. I will follow you to the ends of the earth and haunt you until your dying day."

If Summer hadn't accompanied the cheesy phrase with her version of crazy eyes, I wouldn't have had to hold back a snort. And still, Margo hesitated until Summer thundered, "Confess."

"Fine. I did it. Okay? I killed my husband. I killed Frank."

I asked the burning question. "Why? Everyone seemed to like Frank. Delia told me he brought you yellow roses."

"He ordered Table at Home meals almost every week to give her a night off from cooking," Summer added.

"Yellow roses." Margo shook her head. "I hate yellow roses. They remind me of death. He bought me death flowers, and he never listened when I said I didn't like them."

"You killed him because he didn't bring you the kind of flowers you like?" Maybe she deserved a lifetime of haunting.

"Because he brought me the kind of flowers she liked," Margo bowed her head and said no more.

Who was she?

Summer had begun to shake with the effort to maintain a visible presence. "Why did you kill me?"

"Why did you kill Summer," I repeated for Ernie's benefit. "She didn't do anything to you."

"I needed to make it look like an accident, so I—" Margo trailed off.

"Finish it, Margo, and say my name."

Margo shook her head.

"Say. My. Name." Summer thrust a finger through Margo's throat, and based on the woman's expression, I figured she got a taste of the heebie-jeebies.

"Summer Merryfield. I killed Summer Merryfield."

Ernie stepped out from his hiding place and took Margo into custody. He didn't ask me any questions, but the look on his face said I wasn't off the hook.

He didn't have cuffs in his suit pocket or anything, but she didn't fight him because as he led her away, Summer went along to make sure Margo toed the line.

"That was...." Drew couldn't find his words.

"Awesome," Jacy supplied.

We walked back inside the tent just in time to see Patrea turn and wind up for the bouquet toss. Jacy shoved me into the waiting throng, and I barely regained my footing before Peggy shoved me out of the way, her fingers mere inches from snatching the bundle of flowers out of the air.

Except it wobbled, and then bobbled, and landed right in my arms.

A cheer went up, hands patted me on the back. Not Peggy's, she drilled me with a dirty look and stalked away.

I looked up to see Summer standing next to Patrea. She grinned at me, glanced at Drew, waggled her eyebrows, and waved. Then she was gone.

-The End-